CW01183350

Naked Murder

A Sanford 3rd Age Club Mystery (#25)

David W Robinson

www.darkstroke.com

Copyright © 2022 by David W Robinson
Cover Photography by Adobe Stock © DiViArts
Design by Services for Authors
All rights reserved.

No part of this book may be used or reproduced in any manner whatsoever without written permission of the author or Crooked Cat/darkstroke except for brief quotations used for promotion or in reviews. This is a work of fiction. Names, characters, and incidents are used fictitiously.

First Dark Edition, darkstroke, Crooked Cat Books 2022

Discover us online:
www.darkstroke.com

Find us on instagram:
www.instagram.com/darkstrokebooks

Include **#darkstroke** in a photo of yourself holding this book on Instagram and **something nice will happen.**

The STAC Mystery series:

#1 The Filey Connection
#2 The I-Spy Murders
#3 A Halloween Homicide
#4 A Murder for Christmas
#5 Murder at the Murder Mystery Weekend
#6 My Deadly Valentine
#7 The Chocolate Egg Murders
#8 The Summer Wedding Murder
#9 Costa del Murder
#10 Christmas Crackers
#11 Death in Distribution
#12 A Killing in the Family
#13 A Theatrical Murder
#14 Trial by Fire
#15 Peril in Palmanova
#16 The Squire's Lodge Murders
#17 Murder at the Treasure Hunt
#18 A Cornish Killing
#19 Merry Murders Everyone
#20 A Tangle in Tenerife
#21 Tis The Season To Be Murdered
#22 Confusion in Cleethorpes
#23 Murder on the Movie Set
#24 A Deadly Twixmas

Tales from the Lazy Luncheonette Casebook

By the same author:

#1 A Case of Missing on Midthorpe
#2 A Case of Bloodshed in Benidorm

#1 The Anagramist
#2 The Frame

Acknowledgements

I'm indebted to Ted Bun for his expertise and assistance on naturism which, in the interest of accuracy, helped clarify the rules on a number of issues.

The Author

David Robinson is a Yorkshireman now living in Manchester. Driven by a huge, cynical sense of humour, he's been a writer for over thirty years having begun with magazine articles before moving on to novels and TV scripts.

He has little to do with his life other than write, as a consequence of which his output is prodigious. Thankfully most of it is never seen by the great reading public of the world.

He has worked closely with Crooked Cat Books and darkstroke since 2012, when The Filey Connection, the very first Sanford 3rd Age Club Mystery, was published.

Describing himself as the Doyen of Domestic Disasters he can be found blogging at **www.dwrob.com** and he appears frequently on video (written, produced and starring himself) dispensing his mocking humour at **www.youtube.com/user/Dwrob96/videos**

Naked Murder
A Sanford 3rd Age Club Mystery (#25)

Prologue

Detective Inspector Kirsty Hinch put on her most sympathetic face. "I have to say, Mr Edström, that I'm not hopeful. We will, of course, investigate but I wouldn't back your chances of our coming to a solution other than by pure luck."

Håkan Edström had lived in the UK long enough to be aware of the budgetary constraints under which the police worked and he had not expected anything different to the thin excuse Kirsty gave him. Had he come to the police station to report a murder or ask for an update on an assault inquiry, she would have been more enthusiastic, more positive, assured of a solution somewhere along the line, but theft… It was so commonplace, so frequent that it would probably require a huge task force which the Skegness police simply did not have.

A native of Gothenburg, Sweden, he had spent the last two and a half decades of his fifty years on the Lincolnshire coast, and for most of that time he had been a happy man. It was only with the coming of this summer season that his small holiday park a few miles to the south, had been plagued by frequent thefts, and his members' complaints had become more vociferous.

"If the police can offer no help, can you suggest an alternative course of action?" After so long in the UK, his English was perfect and carried only the faintest trace of his natural Scandinavian brogue.

"Well—"

Edström interrupted before Kirsty could go into whatever it was she was going to say. "I need you to understand, Inspector, that the number and frequency of thefts is likely to cost me members, and as a result, it will affect my income. I appreciate your position, your problems, but if you look at it from my point view, you will see that I have to take some form of action."

"I understand that, Mr Edström, and the only suggestion I can offer is one we've made before: permanent security. It's true that security officers are restricted in the actions they can take. They don't, for example, have the right to search such as we do. But if nothing else, they could restrain a suspect, hold them until we get there."

Edström shook his head. "Given the nature of the Sun Kissed Holiday Park, permanent security, other than that which we have in place at the moment, is not an option. Not unless you could point us at someone who shares our lifestyle choices. Can you suggest anything else?"

Kirsty drummed her fingers on the desktop, allowed her eyes to roam around her small office. Anything to distract her, allow her freewheeling imagination to drop something into the forefront of her mind. The place offered little in the way of such distractions. Staff notices, one or two warnings reminding officers to log out of the police intranet before shutting down computers, and on another wall a poster for an amateur production of King Lear at the Rep Theatre. She had tickets for Thursday evening. Not that she was a great lover of Shakespeare, but her partner was a fan.

The poster called to mind a questionable production of Hamlet which had been staged there a few years back, during which several members of the cast, along with the star of a pantomime staged in Mablethorpe were murdered. That was a tough nut to crack, but enjoyable. Since her promotion to inspector, she had not yet confronted anything so demanding. Instead, she was plagued with the traditional problems of a seaside town in the summer season: shoplifting, general theft, hooliganism, drunken brawls, and of course, drug dealing. Challenging work, but not half so interesting as a murder case.

And it had to be said that were it not for the assistance of an amateur private investigator from somewhere up north, they probably would not have nailed the perpetrator of the

Hamlet murders. She remembered that shabby, antagonistic little man with great fondness. Outspoken, irritating, but with a keen eye, and a brain that was wired up differently, one that could string together the most elusive of clues.

Her memory triggered, she focused on Edström. "There is one thing you could consider, Mr Edström. Bring in a private detective. Working incognito, he could mingle with the members, and the gentleman I'm thinking of is an absolute ace. I could give you his name and I'm sure I still have his number someone." She picked up her mobile phone from the desktop, and began to thumb through the directory. "Chap named Joe Murray," she went on as she searched for his number. "You'd need to offer him accommodation, and I honestly can't swear to it, but I think he's turned professional since the last time I met him, so you would be looking at paying him."

Edström dismissed the comment. "Payment is not an issue, Inspector. If he can get to the bottom of the problem, identify the culprit, I'm more than happy to pay his fees. You say he's from the north. Are you sure he would come all the way to Skegness." Edström looked even more concerned. "Are you sure he would be prepared to work on my park?"

Vicarious images filled Kirsty's mind, and she laughed. "No, I'm not sure. If I were you, I wouldn't go into too much detail, and let him find out for himself when he gets here."

"And if he comes all this way and then refuses to work when he learns about Sun Kissed?"

Kirsty was still trying to control her humour. "Then you refuse to pay."

"You see," Edström pressed on, "no matter what kind of service I want from any individual or organisation, I come up against this same issue."

"I'm sorry, Mr Edström. I can't help you there. All I can do is offer suggestions, such as the one I've just given you." She took off the top sheet of a Post-It pad and scribbled Joe Murray's name and number on it. After checking that she had it right, she handed it across the desk. "Give him a ring. The worst he can do is refuse."

"I will do so, and in the meantime, if you do come across any information which may help us identify the perpetrator, please let me know."

"You can count on it, sir."

Edström came out of the police station into the sweltering, July sunshine, climbed into his car, and pulled out onto the tree-lined carriageway of Park Road, making his way onto the promenade and turning south through Skegness centre. He had less than five miles to go between the multi-storey police station and his little holiday park sheltered away on the coast.

He felt hot and uncomfortable in the plain, white shirt and dark tie, and even the trousers of his lightweight suit, felt damp with sweat. He looked forward to getting back to the Sun Kissed Holiday Park and throwing off all his clothing. Perhaps he would take a swim before lunch. He smiled at the idea. Skinny-dipping, textiles called it, but to him it was perfectly natural, and if he had even the slightest of doubts in his mind, it concerned this Joe Murray. Inspector Hinch may be right about him. An excellent detective he might be, but how would he react to learning the true nature of Sun Kissed Holiday Park?

Chapter One

Joe Murray had stood behind the counter of The Lazy Luncheonette for almost half a century, but there were times when he would be happy to throw off his whites, walk out through the front door and not bother coming back.

It was a transient feeling. The café, one of the most popular in Sanford, might not have made him a wealthy man, but he was better than comfortably off, and with his efforts as a private investigator, he could hardly complain. Well, he could, and he did, but most of Sanford's 50,000 strong population knew to take his grumbles with more than a pinch of salt. Joe Murray was a legend – a grumpy legend.

The fleeting desire to abandon his business, his income, his life's work, usually came with the searing heat of a British summer, especially in July and August when temperatures reached intolerable levels. The heat did nothing to shorten the daily queue of the Sanford Brewery draymen, nor did it minimise the number of clerks, computer operators, executives from the office block around and above the café, calling for breakfast to go. The only difference, so it seemed to Joe, was that in the summer he sold almost as many chilled soft drinks as he did tea, coffee, cappuccino, latte, Americano.

It was a bigger problem in the kitchen where his nephew Lee acted as head chef, assisted by his wife Cheryl, and one of Joe's longest friends, Brenda Jump. Not only did they have to put up with the scorching heat of the day, but also the temperature of the ovens and hobs. The back door was left open, freestanding fans stood in strategic locations, away from the busy areas, but their crossflow made only tiny inroads into the raw heat. Joe was spared that. He stood at the counter taking orders, taking money, giving change, while the other assistants, his good friend Sheila Riley, and the latest addition to the café's crew, Kayleigh Watson, delivered the meals and cleared the tables. The only time Joe moved from the counter was when the queue slackened, at which times he would get out and help Sheila and Kayleigh.

The system worked. The café was never less than busy but with the almost unbearable heat of July adding to the pressure, Joe's eyes strayed to the door and the street beyond, entertaining the faint wish that he could disappear.

Thursday morning was neither more nor less busy than any other day of the week, although the draymen seemed to be in more of a hurry to get through breakfast. The sooner they finished their day's work, the sooner they could clock off, go home, and hide away from the summer heat... or perhaps take in more of it in their back gardens.

This Thursday was a little different. Joe, Sheila, and Brenda would be calling it a day at about half past ten in the morning, and by eleven o'clock they would be in their cars, his and Sheila's, and on their way to the Sun Kissed Holiday Park near Skegness.

The call from Håkan Edström came out of the blue at half past one on Monday afternoon, and after a rambling introduction to himself, Edström told Joe that Inspector Hinch of the Skegness police had recommended him.

The number of timewasters and cold callers had proliferated in line with the ubiquitous technology of mobile phones, and Joe was ever wary of unsolicited calls. Harbouring the slight suspicion that Håkan Edström was one such, Joe went on the defensive. "I don't think I know an Inspector Hinch."

"Apparently you helped her clear up some nasty killings at the Rep Theatre a couple of years ago."

The light dawned in Joe's overheated mind and he dismissed any doubts of Edström's bona fides. "Oh. The Hamlet murders, and you're talking about Kirsty Hinch. She was a sergeant back then. I imagine she was promoted on the back of the help I gave them with that business at the Rep." An arrogant assumption but Joe had never been shy about taking the credit, real or imaginary, for his skills.

"Perhaps," Håkan agreed. "Whatever the reason, she has moved up the ranks, and she suggested I give you a call. I need the services of a private investigator. She recommended you."

Doubt set in Joe's mind once more. "It's not that I mind, but it's about cost. It's going to set you back a bob or two. I live a good hundred and something miles from Skegness. And then there's the cost of accommodation, and other incidental expenses. That's all over and above my hourly or daily charge."

"Please, Mr Murray, I am getting desperate. I'll pay whatever you ask. I can afford it. I own the Sun Kissed Holiday Park, and we are being targeted by thieves. Inspector Hinch has made it clear that although the police will do what they can, they cannot prioritise our problems. Accommodation is not a problem. I have chalets available on the park, but there is something I must—"

The prospect interested Joe from the off, and he interrupted Edström. "One thing. It's not just me you'll need to accommodate. I'll be bringing my two assistants, Sheila Riley and Brenda Jump."

"Once again, that is not a problem. I can arrange a two-bedroom chalet. But—"

Yet again, Joe cut him off. "It'll take me a day or two to organise things at this end. If we turn up mid Thursday afternoon, would that suit you?"

"Yes. But there is something I must tell you—"

Joe interrupted for the third time. "I'm in the middle of a day's work here, boss, so tell me when we get there on Thursday. In the meantime, let me spell out my charges."

Barely giving Edström the chance to say anything, Joe went on to detail his rates (by the day rather than the hour) and guarantees (none), and several times during the call, Edström tried to interrupt, but Joe, his head filled with images of sunny days by the seaside and a serious amount of money coming in, did not give him the opportunity. Soon afterwards, with Edström no longer bothering to even make the effort at getting a word in, Joe rang off, and proceeded to spell out the situation to Sheila and Brenda, and then consulted the other crew members who would have to run The Lazy Luncheonette while he and the two women were away.

As always, he anticipated a lot of ribbing from the draymen of Sanford Brewery, and from the following morning, when he announced it, they did not let him down.

"Skegness?" asked Barry Standish with a humorous gleam in his eyes. "You don't half know how to live, don't you, Joe? I meanersay, some of us have to slum it in Benidorm or Mykonos, or the Canaries, but you go for the height of decadence in Skeggy."

Wondering where Barry might have learned a word like 'decadence', Joe quipped, "We got tired of St Tropez." He took Barry's money and rang up the sale of a full English breakfast.

"What happened to those Americans who were supposed to be visiting us?" Barry asked. "Les Tanner mentioned them and it was in the papers."

"They had to cancel," Joe explained as he handed over change. "Hangover from the Covid crisis or something. Made me look a right bloody fool after all the trouble I went to, arranging a civic reception and stuff."

"Oh, I shouldn't think you'd need America's help to look a right bloody fool. Most of the time you manage it on your own."

If the draymen took the mickey, Joe was comfortable in the knowledge that The Lazy Luncheonette was safe for the time he and his two friends would be on the Lincolnshire coast. Whenever Joe and two women took time away from the business, Lee, Cheryl, and Kayleigh, along with the assistance of occasional casuals, took over the running of the café, and the procedures were so ingrained that there were rarely any hiccups.

"You can trust us, Uncle Joe," Lee said when the situation position was spelled out. "You three get off to Sketch Mess and don't worry about The Lazy Luncheonette."

Joe often wondered just how Lee could manage to get minor details like the name of the town so wrong. There again, it had been going on for most the twenty-eight year old, former rugby player's life, so no one questioned it for long. Even his wife, Cheryl, simply accepted it. Kayleigh was much like Lee, and often misunderstood or misinterpreted the words of friends, family, workmates and customers, but in both cases, they were cheerful, reliable members of the crew, and it was left to the equally cheerful Cheryl to organise matters when the three senior members were absent.

Summer was also the worst of times. Kayleigh would be going away on holiday with her family very soon, Lee and Cheryl had booked a week in Great Yarmouth for early in August, and towards the end of that month, Joe himself would be making for Tenerife and a week-long visit with his ex-wife. The moment he got back, Sheila and Brenda would be flying off to Cyprus for a week.

In terms of staff levels, The Lazy Luncheonette ran on a shoestring, and it took planning on an almost military scale to cover the various staff absences. Fortunately, he had a small reservoir of reliable casuals he could call on, not least of whom was Pauline Watson, Kayleigh's elder sister.

All that aside, with the arrangements made, Joe was actively looking forward to a few days in Skegness, even though he recalled the place with no particular fondness. That was down to the time of year – early January – when they last visited. Cold, raining, and complicated by several nasty murders.

During Tuesday and Wednesday, whether behind the counter in The Lazy Luncheonette or in the bar of the Miners Arms, he waxed raw enthusiasm about the forthcoming visit, making sure everyone knew how much he (and Sheila and Brenda) were looking forward to the break at the Sun Kissed Holiday Park.

If there was any puzzle, it came on Wednesday evening, when he was at the bar, and he noticed Brenda talking to one of her infrequent men friends, George Robson. A stalwart of the 3rd Age Club, there had been an on and off relationship between the pair for many years. George, along with his pal Owen Frickley, was notorious for his womanising, a factor which contributed to his divorce.

This was different. Brenda and George appeared to be sharing a joke, one which George found hilarious, but when Joe asked, Brenda refused to say anything beyond, "Mind your own business."

Joe spent much of Wednesday night packing his small suitcase. Putting in this shirt, that jumper, those trousers, and then throwing it out again after checking the weather and the news that temperatures were rising and the present heatwave was not expected to end for at least another five or six days. Whatever the complications of Håkan Edström's problems, surely they would have it cracked before then?

On Thursday morning he arrived at The Lazy Luncheonette a little after six, with his minimal clothing packed and secure in the boot of his car. When Sheila and Brenda turned up at seven, he took their luggage, at least three times the size and amount that he was taking, into his car.

And now, with their departure imminent, Joe ran through the routines for the last time, until Cheryl grew sick of hearing him and said, "Get in your car and go, Joe. We know what we're doing. Go sort this bloke's knicker nicker out and then enjoy yourselves for a few days."

"Enjoy ourselves? In Skegness?" Joe frowned. "And who mentioned anything about thieving underwear?"

"Is there a proper name for an underwear thief?" Sheila asked. "Something Like pantiklepto?"

Brenda giggled. "A frill seeker?"

Cheryl laughed along with them.

"No one is nicking knickers," Joe protested

"He must be," Cheryl objected. "Why else would this nurk send for you? If the tealeaf was stealing wallets and purses and stuff, he'd get the police in, wouldn't he?"

"Yeah but the police—"

"Joe," Brenda interrupted, "let's get moving. It's pushing eleven o'clock, the roads will be bad enough, and we have a hundred and odd miles in front of us."

Chapter Two

Joe knew when he was beaten and led the way out through the rear door to his car and checked that the small suitcase and two larger ones belonging to the women, along with a cold box containing basic food supplies, were secure. They would follow in Sheila's Fiat.

He had spent the last three days sorting out the route and committing it to memory. "Try to keep up with me if you can," he said. "M62, M18, M180 all the way to Grimsby, and from there it's the A something or other south for Lincoln-ish and Skeggy."

"A something or other. Gotta love your precision, Joe," Brenda commented. "Didn't it have a number?"

"I forget. If we get separated, I'll stop where I can and you can bell me."

Sheila was more practical. "Well, don't go flying away at ninety miles an hour."

This time, Brenda laughed. "Ninety miles an hour? Joe's old wreck. He's hard pressed to get it up to thirty."

"It'll still be going when you're past it, Brenda," Joe grumbled.

"It's going to have to go some then," Sheila said. "Brenda is showing no signs of slowing down."

A couple of minutes later, they pulled out from the rear of The Lazy Luncheonette, ran south along Doncaster Road, and joined the M62, turning east for the A1, Doncaster, and Hull.

Brenda was only part right. The traffic would eventually pick up on what was one of the busiest stretches of roads in the country during the summer months, but at this hour, it was no worse than moderate. In deference to Sheila's demands, he kept his speed down to a conservative 55-60, with frequent checks in the mirror to ensure they were keeping pace with him, and he savoured the exquisite pleasure of an open road and the prospect of a pleasant, two-hour drive with the sun beaming down from a cloudless sky.

It was an alien feeling to him. Other people, those employed rather than self-employed, enjoyed this freedom every time they went away for a holiday. A break from routine, no boss looking over their shoulder for a week or two, a change of scenery, the prospect of doing exactly as they pleased for the duration of the vacation. It was different for Joe. Even when he travelled abroad, Tenerife to see his ex-wife, or holidays in one of the Balearics or mainland Spain, The Lazy Luncheonette was never far from his thoughts, and he would ring regularly during his absence to ensure things were going smoothly.

They were never anything but. Cheryl and Lee, and to a lesser extent Kayleigh, all knew what they were doing, and the only time matters had been any different was that fateful Easter weekend in Blackpool when an arsonist burned down the old café.

For all that they were junior partners in the business, entitled to a share of the quarterly profits, Sheila, Brenda, and Lee forgot about the place when they were on holiday. The two women would fly off to Cyprus in the next few weeks, and Joe could guarantee that aside from the occasional multimedia text carrying photographs of their hotel and surrounding area, he would hear nothing from them, and even when he did, they would never mention The Lazy Luncheonette.

A little over an hour after leaving Sanford, still fifteen miles shy of Grimsby, he pulled into a service station on the outskirts of Brigg, where the M180 ceased to be a motorway and became the A180.

"This is the life," Brenda said as they settled with a fresh cup of tea and a snack at a wooden picnic table outside the cafeteria. "Why couldn't I meet a multimillionaire and spend all my time like this?"

A sarcastic fire came to Joe's eyes. "What? You want to hook up with a millionaire and all he can do is take you on trips to Grimsby and Skegness? No wonder he's a millionaire."

"Bog off, you. You know what I mean."

Bringing a little educated common sense to the debate, ensuring it didn't drift into a farcical trading of light insults, Sheila said, "I don't think money's that important. As long as you look forward to your destination, and I have to say that I'm seriously looking forward to Skegness and the Sun Kissed Holiday Park."

Joe was in no mood for seriousness. "Yes, well, you should watch out for Håkan Edström. He's Swedish, and you know what they're like about persuading their womenfolk."

"Oh, I know," Brenda said, and laughed.

Sheila gave her a curious look, and a more irritated one at Joe. "I don't think they're any different to the British. Perhaps a little freer in their attitude, but even so, Mr Edström can try all he likes. It won't get him anywhere with me."

Again, Brenda gave a naughty chuckle. "You speak for yourself, Sheila Riley."

After a half hour stopover, their lunchtime appetites satisfied, they visited the toilet, and then pulled onto the petrol pumps to fill the tanks on both cars.

"On my credit card," Joe complained after paying for all the petrol.

Brenda gave him a mock-sweet smile. "You did invite us along, Joe, so it seems only right that you should stump up for the travel expenses."

"Not me. Håkan Edström. I'll add it to his bill."

"Well, in that case, stop moaning and let get moving."

Battling their way through the outskirts and around the centre of Grimsby, Joe was reminded of a weekend in nearby Cleethorpes the previous year. Although they enjoyed the break, it was fraught with difficulties of one kind or another, and Joe came as close as ever to resigning the Chair of the Sanford 3rd Age Club. It was as that weekend came to a close that Sheila persuaded him that he should put his investigative efforts on a professional footing, and after their return, he took the necessary courses to become a fully licensed private eye. She persuaded him that the money he made from his investigations would offset the level of stress, and that was fine in theory, but in practice, he had so few calls that his income was negligible, although he did secure quite a bit of work with North Shires Insurance... work he had before he invested all that money in securing his licence.

They lost several minutes fighting with the traffic through Grimsby, after which they followed the A16 to the south, and before they had left the town, the dual carriageway ended, leaving them with approximately 40 miles of single carriageway, some of it wide enough to facilitate overtaking heavy lorries or slow-moving agricultural vehicles, but often too narrow and too busy to maintain momentum. As a consequence, it was getting on for half past one before they arrived on Skegness seafront, where Joe once again stopped so they could enjoy a cup of tea and savour the sunshine and the tang of coastal ozone.

Spread before them, the beach was busy, the fairground, and from the various arcades and amusement centres came the recognisable whistles, beeps, and snatches of familiar tunes emanating from slot machines.

"Perishing cold the last time we came here," Brenda commented.

"Yes, but it was New Year, dear," Sheila replied. "We were here for that production of Hamlet, weren't we? The one with young Teri Sanford playing Ophelia."

"Yes, by the time we were done, we had more real-life bodies than they did in the play," Joe said.

"But you solved it, didn't you," Brenda said. "A proper little Sherlock, you were."

"Aren't I always?" Joe grinned at her. "Actually, Brenda, it was as much to do with you two as it was with me. You confirmed that the suicide note was nothing of the kind."

Sheila was a sudden flurry of excitement. "Oh yes, I remember." Right away her face fell. "What a sad set of people they were."

"It's the way of the world," Joe said. "I swear it gets dirtier every day." He glanced at his watch. "Shall we make a move?"

"Is it far now, Joe?"

"About four miles, according to my satnav. Somewhere near Gibraltar Point Nature Reserve. The place must be pretty exclusive. Looking at it on Google Maps, it's tucked away in woodland, just off the beach."

While a smirk crossed Brenda's face, Sheila was more enthusiastic. "Very posh. I can hardly wait to see it."

From their parking spot, the route involved cutting back in towards the town centre, then turning south along a busy, suburban road, until the houses petered out and they were back in, not exactly open countryside, but certainly an area less heavily populated, with housing on one side of the road only, the side furthest from the shore. They passed a golf course, and the road narrowed to a single track. Further on, they came to the signs for the Gibraltar Point Nature Reserve, after which, Joe slowed down even further, looking for the entrance to the Sun Kissed Holiday Park.

It came upon him so suddenly and was so shrouded in the lower branches of surrounding trees that he almost missed it, and he had to brake sharply, bringing a blast from Sheila's horn, before he swung into the gate.

He and Sheila were busy remonstrating with each other, Sheila gesticulating through her windscreen, Joe ranting via his mirror, and neither of them noticed the small print on the sign. Keeping his speed down to a ten mph crawl, he followed the narrow, winding track, until suddenly it opened out into a parking area, with few vehicles in evidence. He guessed that if the place was as busy as Edström had suggested on the phone, those paths leading away from this small building, had to be accessible by car, and the guests' vehicles would be parked outside their individual chalets.

He climbed out of the car, lit a cigarette, and took a deep, satisfying drag.

"This is what it's all about," he said. "Let's hope we can crack the case quickly, and have a few days to ourselves."

Sheila agreed with a nod, but he noticed that Brenda had a faint smirk on her face again.

Joe noticed it too. "Did I say something funny?"

That wiped the smile from Brenda's lips. "Oh no. I'm like you, Joe. Just pleased to be here instead of stuffy old Sanford."

"Aren't we all… Oh my lord."

Sheila's exclamation pulled Joe's attention. "What? What is it?"

She pointed frantically to her right, and one of the narrow paths Joe had noticed. "A man walking along there. I swear he was naked."

Joe followed her pointing finger and could see no one. "A drunken streaker, probably. You know what these places are like." As he spoke, Brenda laughed aloud. "What's wrong with you, woman?"

"Nothing," Brenda said barely able to suppress her laughter. "I'm just thinking, Sheila seeing naked men. You're sure it's not just wishful thinking, dear?"

Sheila looked down her nose at her best friend. "You're walking on eggshells, Brenda."

Joe headed off the potential argument. "Yeah, well, let's get inside and see this guy."

He led the way into the reception hut, found no one in attendance, and rang the bell on the counter. "Not as busy as they claimed," he said.

At once, a woman he guessed to be in her late forties or early fifties, emerged from the rear office and Joe gaped. She was completely naked, and when she reached the counter, her breasts remained proudly displayed, almost resting on it. "Good afternoon, and welcome to the Sun Kissed Holiday Park."

Sheila's face shone red as a traffic light, Joe was dumbfounded, unable to speak, and Brenda could control herself no longer. She all but collapsed in fits of laughter.

"I'm Margot Edström. How can I help you?"

"I… er…" Joe was still struggling to find words. "I… Don't you think you should put some clothes on?"

"Whatever for?"

"Well, see, where we come from—"

"Oh, you're textiles aren't you? And you've taken a wrong turn, haven't you?"

Averting his eyes, Joe continued speaking to her. "Textiles? Do I look like a sheet of curtain material?"

"Don't tempt the lady into giving you an answer you might not like, Joe," Brenda giggled.

Ignoring her, Joe went on to Margot. "We're expected. Joe Murray and colleagues. Private investigators from Sanford."

"Ah. Wait there a minute, Mr Murray, and I'll get my husband."

She disappeared into the rear office, and Edström appeared, every bit as naked as his wife. "Mr Murray, I'm very pleased to meet you. Håkan Edström, proprietor of the Sun Kissed Holiday Park." He offered his hand and Joe shook it with some reluctance.

Sheila was still blushing, Brenda was still laughing, and Joe was still gobsmacked. He fell back on his lifelong habit of speaking his mind. "Doesn't anyone around here wear clothes?"

"Why would they?" Edström asked.

"Well, it is traditional."

"Not here it isn't. Sun Kissed, Mr Murray, is a naturist resort."

Chapter Three

Sheila's face seemed to glow even redder, Brenda could hardly control her laughter, and Joe was fit to explode when he finally responded to Edström's announcement. "A naturist site? You never said anything on the phone."

"With respect, Mr Murray, I tried to tell you several times, but you wouldn't let me get a word in."

Getting some control over her mirth, Brenda said, "And if you'd looked at the noticeboard when you turned in, Joe, you would have known. But you were too busy arguing with Sheila through your mirror." She turned to Sheila. "And you were too busy complaining about him to notice."

Sheila's colour now signalled her anger. "You mean you knew?"

Brenda nodded. "Why do you think I've been giggling since you saw that naked man?" Once again she dissolved into fits of uncontrollable laughter. "Oh dear. If I don't stop it, I'll wet myself."

Edström was joined by his wife, who asked, "Is there some problem?"

Preferring to concentrate on Brenda rather than the park proprietors, Joe's annoyance rose further. "Why didn't you say something while we were outside?"

"Why should I? It doesn't bother me... Well, close up it might bother me, but close up I can always turn the lights out."

Joe focused on Edström's face, ensuring that he kept Mrs Edström in his peripheral vision. "That's it. We're leaving."

He turned to march out of the hut, but Edström stayed him. "Please, Mr Murray, we need your help. If it makes you feel any more comfortable, my wife and I will put on robes."

It seemed to Joe that Sheila was in complete agreement with him, but Brenda was concentrated on a more important issue. "They need our help, Joe, and I'm sure Mr Edström won't ask you to take your clothes off." She half turned away and still chuckling to herself, muttered as an aside, "At least, we hope not."

He faced Edström once more. "I'll listen to you. No guarantees."

Ten minutes later, the five of them were ensconced in the rear office, which was barely large enough to accommodate them.

Both Margot and Edström wore thin bathrobes, loosely tied at the waist, although Joe noticed that when Margot crossed her legs, her pink robe had a habit of sliding off to one side, bearing most of her chunky thighs and other areas which Joe found disturbing, often causing him to look away until the lady put her attire right.

Sheila was still uncomfortable, Brenda appeared totally relaxed, and Joe compelled himself to focus on business. Margot served tea, and Edström ran into his story.

"I am Swedish by birth, but I have lived in your country for over twenty-five years, ever since I first met Margot and persuaded her to become my wife." At that point Edström took hold of his wife's hand causing her robe to slip once more. "Not long after we moved here, we set up Sun Kissed. The park was designed for others of the same persuasion as ourselves. In other words, nature lovers. In common with most naturist parks, Sun Kissed is officially described as clothing optional. Our members dress for dinner, our kitchen staff are clothed. They have to be from both a health and safety and hygiene point of view. Our bar staff, only one man and one woman are also clothed. In other words, Mr Murray, nudity is not compulsory but acceptance of nudity is. To put it bluntly, our guests enjoy freedom of choice, and most of them are quite happy to remain as nature intended. We are, as you've probably realised, well-shielded from… How would I describe them? Sightseers."

"You mean nosy parkers?" Brenda suggested.

"An English idiom which describes such people perfectly, Mrs Jump. So not only do we enjoy our freedom to be without clothing, but we also enjoy absolute privacy."

Joe was beginning to tire of what he saw as a sales pitch. "Is all this leading somewhere, Mr Edström?"

"Please call me Håkan, and my wife is Margot."

"Fine. I'm Joe, this is Sheila, this is Brenda. Now, as I asked, is all this going somewhere or are you simply trying to persuade us to strip off?"

"Quite the opposite, Joe. I said that Sun Kissed is clothing optional. In other words, you do not have to remove your clothing. Our members might be more comfortable in your presence if you reduce the amount you wear, and the weather is excellent for, say, shorts and a T-shirt, or shorts and no T-shirt, and in the case of the ladies, perhaps a swimming costume."

"Right. So we've cleared that up. That doesn't cure our, erm… what's the word? Discomfort in dealing with people who are in the altogether."

Margot chuckled. "Discomfort? Do you mean embarrassment, Mr Murray?"

Joe laid a steely eye on her. "It takes a lot to embarrass me, Margot, so no, I really do mean discomfort. You see, you haven't gone into the details of your problem yet, other than what Håkan told me over the phone. Theft, you said. At some stage, we will have to speak to your members and we're likely to find that kind of situation uncomfortable."

"Hear hear," Sheila muttered.

Brenda's response was even quieter. "You speak for yourself, Joe Murray."

Edström was quick to remind Joe of Tuesday's phone call. "Had you not been so eager to take on the work and put across your charges over the telephone, Mr Murray, you would have been aware of all this."

"Yeah, yeah, yeah. I know. I have a big mouth."

"You can say that again," Brenda said in a normal tone, and focused on Edström. "There's a simple solution to this, Håkan. Make it clear to your members that there are private investigators at work, and when we speak to them, ask them to pay due deference to our situation and wear robes, similar to the ones you and your wife are wearing." Edström would have commented, but Brenda pressed on. "I'm not quite so prim and narrow minded as my two friends, and I will not denounce your lifestyle because I believe in the freedom of the individual, and somewhere deep down, I'm certain that both Joe and Sheila are with me on that. So, Margot, ignore Joe. I think you called it right. They are embarrassed."

"Thank you for nothing, Brenda," Sheila said before facing the park proprietors. "Yes, I do find it uncomfortable and more than a little embarrassing, but as Joe has already said, if you can arrange for your members to be at least partially clothed when we speak to them, I'm sure we'll cope."

"I will explain the situation to our members, but please understand, it is the individual's choice. If they choose to dress, if only in a bathrobe, then fine, if they choose to remain without clothing, then you will have to deal with that situation." Edström sipped at his tea. "To clarify the situation, using nudity for the purpose of intentional harassment, alarm, or distress is an offence under section 4A of the Public Order Act, but Sun Kissed is a private, secluded, members' only site, and we therefore commit no crime here. That seclusion would not be our choice, but it's a necessity to keep at bay the nosy parkers as Mrs Jump described them, and of course, the media, which takes great pleasure in gratuitous nonsense."

"We can carry on yattering like this all day," Joe complained. "And telling your members we're private eyes won't cut it. We should be working incognito."

"We should be working in the nuddy," Brenda muttered, and could not supress a chuckle.

"Shut up, Brenda, or I'll insist that you strip first." Joe turned back to the Edströms. "Can we get to the nitty-gritty of your problem?"

"Theft, Joe, as I explained on the telephone. The persistent theft of our members' personal effects: money, mobile telephones, laptop computers, tablets, even a few cameras, both still and video, which people had stowed away in their luggage." Håkan smiled. "Use of cameras is not permitted on site. It's been going on for about three months. As a matter of routine, all thefts are reported to the police, but when I spoke to Inspector Hinch on Monday morning, she was not hopeful of a solution, which is why she suggested I call you."

Joe sank into contemplative silence. He could not pretend to himself or to the Edströms that this would be an easy case to crack, and the fact that they were on a naturist site only aggravated his thought processes on the way ahead. On the other hand, he enjoyed, if that was the correct word, an innate sense of justice, of right and wrong. Regardless of their esoteric choices, people were being systematically robbed, and he knew from personal experience how distressing that could be. He would need many more details, no matter how uncomfortable the process of securing the data.

And it was not as if he had any personal objections to naturism. As Brenda had said, it was a matter of freedom of choice, and these people were free to choose how they spent their leisure time. It just wasn't for him personally. He was fine with nudity, but it was restricted to the bathroom, and on occasion the bedroom (usually with the lights off).

"Has anything happened this week?" he asked.

Edström nodded. "There have been three incidents his week. Mr Welsby and his partner, Ms Simpson suffered a break-in on Tuesday afternoon, during which an expensive, gents' wristwatch and Ms Simpson's purse were stolen. A second couple and a gentleman holidaying alone also suffered break-ins."

"We'll need to speak to them," Joe said and sank into his thoughts again.

Before he could announce any conclusion, Sheila spoke up again, but she spoke first to Joe. "You're getting this wrong. None of us are naturists and that would make us stand out amongst the guests. We should not be working undercover, and Mr Edström should inform everyone who we are and why we're here."

Before Joe could tackle her, Brenda came down on her best friend's side. "She's right, Joe. If we try to pretend we're anything other than what we are, we'll stand out like a spare —"

"Right. Right." Joe admitted defeat. "However you want to play it."

Sheila now addressed the park owners. "I have to say, Mr and Mrs Edström, that I can see your situation, and I'm sure we can help, but I would insist that Joe, Brenda, and I stay at a nearby hotel. Your analysis, Mrs Edström, was probably correct. I feel very uncomfortable in such an environment, but far from embarrassment, my main concern is that my discomfort will cloud my judgement." She cast a disdainful glance at Brenda. "I can't speak for my best friend here, but I believe Joe might feel the same way."

Edström disagreed. "It's the height of the season, and I think you would be very lucky to secure rooms anywhere. Permit me to make a suggestion. We have arranged accommodation for you, a two-bedroom chalet. Why not spend the night there, and then check out local hotels tomorrow morning?"

"Fine by me," Brenda said.

"If that's how it has to be, I suppose that is how it will have to be," Sheila agreed with obvious reluctance.

"Let's put that to one side for the moment," Joe said. "Have you logged all the incidents? I'll need dates, times, whatever circumstances you're aware of, and assuming that the majority of the victims are not on site today, I'll need contact details so I can ring them and speak to them over the telephone."

Edström stood, causing his robe to fall open. Sheila and Joe looked away, Brenda made no effort to do anything of the kind. Pulling the robe about him, tying the waist strap, he moved behind the desk, slid open the top drawer of a filing cabinet and rifled through the folders until he found the one he was seeking, whereupon he returned to his seat, and handed it to Joe.

"Everything is in there. A total of seventeen thefts over a

period of, I believe, ten weeks. Naturally, Sun Kissed Holiday Park is like any other hotel or caravan park on the coast. We do not accept responsibility for our guests' personal effects, and we stress that they should take care of their own property."

It rang bells in Joe's lively mind, recalling Gittings Caravan Park on the outskirts of Hayle, Cornwall, which had also been the target of thieves, and one victim was Les Tanner. During their week-long stay, Tanner had foolishly left an expensive camera in his caravan, and it went missing. Joe was the one who found it and ensured its eventual return to its owner.

Edström was still talking. "We have run this business for over twenty years now, and we have never had this kind of problem in the past. While we may be able to disclaim responsibility, it does our reputation no favours, and I foresee a downturn in bookings unless we can resolve the issue."

Joe strummed his lips with his fingers. "You describe your guests as 'members'. From that, I take it that you don't cater for, sort of, ad hoc, occasional visitors?"

"Nothing of the kind. We welcome anyone, even those who do not favour naturism, provided they accept our way of life. Photography, whether still or video, is strictly banned. No one is allowed to use cameras on site. It's too easy for such images to appear on social media or sites like YouTube. You see, Joe, many people, perhaps you included, link naturism with sex and that is not the case."

"Well, you are Swedish." Joe didn't mean to say it. It was at the forefront of his mind, a typecast image of the Scandinavians' more open attitude to such matters. "My apologies. I let my mouth run away before I put my brain into gear."

"It's a common enough problem," Brenda commented.

Håkan ignored her. "No apologies necessary. It's true that my fellow countrymen tend to be not so inhibited as the British. To get back to what I was saying, it seems to me that you link naturism with sex, and in fact, it has nothing to do with it. I repeat what I've said so often, Joe, ours is a lifestyle choice. We prefer to be unencumbered with clothing."

"Right. I get that. But you didn't answer my question on membership."

Edström did not hesitate. "Most caravan parks, holiday parks, charge additional fees so that guests may enjoy the restaurants, bar areas, and so on. In our case, we charge a nominal fee – twenty-five pounds – and for the duration of their stay, all guests become members and are bound by the membership code, which encapsulates the acceptance of nudity, but does not insist upon it. Some of our people are what I would describe as permanent members. It is an option. They pay an annual fee of two hundred and fifty pounds, and that entitles them to generous discounts on chalet rentals, free admission to our frequent fancy dress and themed evenings. For example, we are holding a seventies evening next weekend. Now, if you and your two lady friends wished to attend, it would cost you twenty pounds each. The same applies to any transient members. But if you took permanent membership, you would not have to pay anything."

Joe pursed his lips. "It must be an administrative nightmare."

"The administration is what my wife and I are all about. May I ask why you are so interested? Are you considering membership?"

"Not bloody likely." Once again, Joe's mouth ran away with him before he could stop it and he apologised for the second time. "No. Nothing of the kind. I'm simply trying to establish the arrangements, and it boils down to how much you know about your guests. I mean, if someone applied for membership, what do you need to know about them?"

"Name, address, age – members must be eighteen years old or over – occupation – we have to be certain we're not harbouring investigative reporters – and contact details. What else would we need to know? If you were staying at a hotel and they began to pry into your background, how would you react?"

"I'd tell them to get stuffed and then I'd go somewhere else."

"Precisely." Edström seemed to feel he had made his point. "Is there anything else?"

"Yes. The files you hold on your guests, er, members, and your staff."

Edström stood again. "I am reluctant to hand these over. I have your assurance that they will be well-protected?"

"Guaranteed," Joe said.

Edström returned to the desk and passed a bundle of files to Joe, but before he released them, he insisted, "Now, I must ask you to make up your mind. You've detailed your charges, and I accept them, although we will need an itemised bill for expenses. Decision time, Mr Murray. Are you willing to help us?"

Joe looked to his two friends, both of whom returned the slightest of nods. "You've got a deal, Håkan."

Edström got to his feet. "Good. Here is what I suggest. I will escort you to your accommodation." He smiled on Sheila. "Even if it is for one night only. And afterwards, I shall call the members together in the bar and explain the situation to them. And it would be useful, Mr Murray, if at least one of you could be there to clarify any issues which may arise."

"I'll do it if you like," Brenda volunteered and pointed at her companions. "Anything to spare their blushes."

Chapter Four

All three were surprised at how large the site was. From the car park, they could not see beyond the reception block but when Edström led them from reception and through the bar area, it emerged onto an open area with about thirty chalets arranged in a semi-circle around a swimming pool where sunbathers, most of them without clothing, took their ease.

Edström explained that the track from the car park diverged and led to rear of the chalets on both sides where, as Edström explained, the guests parked their cars, and the building from which they emerged stood at the apex of the semicircle. "The bar, as you've just seen, and the adjacent dining room," Edström told them. "As I told you, guests dress for dinner, but during the day, they are free to use the bar without dressing."

"How well do you know the guests?"

"I know some of them quite well. They are like friends. Full members, and come back to us twice, three times, sometimes as many as six times a year." Edström smiled. "Naturism is not limited to the summer months, Joe. It is a conviction, a way of life, and it pays little regard to the changing of the seasons." He waved around the chalets. "We have, perhaps, ten families with us at the moment who are short-stay. That is to say, they're here for the week, and many of them go home on Saturday."

"And these short-stay wallahs, do you know any of them? In other words, have they been here before, and if so, were they here at the time of the thefts?"

"In one or two instances, it is possible, but the lady over there, for example—" He aimed his index finger at a dark haired woman, who had passed them carrying a glass of what looked like cola, and was now ambling towards a sun lounger where she eventually made herself comfortable. A flash of recognition shot through Joe's mind, but Edström was still talking. "Delia Coll. She's a doctor from somewhere in your part of the world. Yorkshire. We've never seen her before. She's been here a week and is scheduled to stay for a second week. That is how it is, Joe. There are those people we know, regular visitors, prominent members, and those we have never seen before and may very well never see again. We are no different to any other holiday park in the country, except that we – and most of our visitors – prefer to relax without clothing. It's rare that we're troubled by textiles such as yourselves, and if it were not for the purpose of solving our problems, I doubt that you would ever have come anywhere near us."

His announcement caught Brenda's attention. "That's the second time we've been called textiles. Your wife used the word earlier when she thought we were lost. Textiles?"

"Our word for people who do not share our belief in naturism, Mrs Jump. It's less insulting than the epithets some textiles used to describe us."

"Live and let live, that's my motto," Brenda said. "Even so, I don't think I could be persuaded to share your enthusiasm."

"And we all know why, don't we?" Joe cast a pointed glanced at her expanding midriff to highlight his unspoken opinion.

Brenda scowled. "At least I don't disappear stood sideways to a lamp post."

Edström opened the front door to chalet #17, led the way in, and handed the key to Joe.

"You'll find everything you need in here. There is a small kitchen, with crockery and cutlery, but if you intend eating in your chalet, I'm afraid the nearest shop is a couple of miles away. On the other hand, you'll find our dining room is adequately set up for all meals and snacks." Edström waved at the room. "There are two bedrooms, a double and a twin, sufficient to cater for a family of four."

Joe looked around and approved. The furnishings were recent and far from cheap. A large screen TV set hung on one wall, there was a comfortable, three seater settee, a couple of armchairs, and a small table where they could take meals or snacks. The front window enjoyed a view over the pool (which he and Sheila purposely avoided) and beyond the rear door on the far side of the small kitchen, there was enough parking for both their cars.

Edström broke into his musings. "And now, if you'll excuse me, I have to call a meeting of the members. Shall we say half past three in the bar?"

Joe and Brenda nodded, Sheila did not respond, and as Edström opened the door, preparing to leave, he paused. "Those files, Mr Murray. You will take care of them? If anything happens to them, we could be liable under the Data Protection Act."

Joe was concerned that Håkan had just announced it to anyone listening in from nearby. "Stop worrying. They'll be safe enough with us."

Håkan left, and the moment the door closed behind him, Sheila called her two friends to order. "I'm sorry, but I can't stay here."

"It's only for the one night, Sheila," Brenda said.

"No. I'm sorry. I can't do it. Even walking from reception was a nightmare." Sheila shuddered. "I cannot countenance all this... this... nudity. Aside from anything else, it's unhygienic, I mean, all those bare bottoms on the furniture, I can't—"

Joe interrupted. "That's me changing my order for dinner."

Brenda frowned. "How so?"

"I fancied rump steak but it's gone off me now."

It was an attempt to lighten the mood. In response, Brenda roared with laughter, and Joe would swear he saw the trace of a smile on Sheila's lips before she brought the discussion back on track.

"Why don't you two stay here, I'll get in my car and make my way back towards Skegness. I'm sure I'll find a B&B where I can lodge."

"It won't alter anything, Sheila," Joe said. "We've agreed to take the case on, and we will have to confront these people, clothed or not."

"I've thought about that, Joe. In fact, I've been thinking about little else since we first agreed to help the Edströms. Let me make a suggestion. The files that Håkan gave you. Let me take them. I have my iPad with me. While you work on the practicalities here, I can deal with the background research wherever I'm staying, and we can meet on neutral ground every day." Her face fell. "Let's be honest about this, you two are handling the, er, ambience much better than me."

Joe cast a glance at Brenda who nodded. "All right. I'll come with you back to the car park so I can give you your suitcase. But before you go, Edström said there had been three incidents this week and he gave us a couple of names – which I forget. Simsby and Welson or something. Before you leave, can you and Brenda skim through the list of thefts and pick them out?"

"Yes. No problem."

Ten minutes later the job was done. While the women made notes of the most recent thefts, Joe skimmed through the files, each of which carried a head and shoulders photograph and thanks to his near-eidetic memory, logged them in his head.

Sheila took the files and as they prepared to leave, Joe advised her, "Wherever you check in, don't forget the bill. We'll need to charge Edström for it. You're okay with all this, Brenda?"

Again she concurred. "Fine. In fact, I'm surprised you're not going with her, Joe."

"Whatever problems I have with these people are not a patch on the problems they'll have with me."

Brenda chuckled. "Remember, we bought tea bags, milk and sugar with us. They're in the cold box in your car, Joe, and you'll need to give some of the gear to Sheila."

"Well that'll mean…" Joe trailed off as an idea struck him. "Now there's a thought, Sheila. There's no reason why you can't join me and Brenda here. By driving your car round the back of the chalets, you'll miss most of the skin on show, and me and Brenda'll deal with this meeting."

"Very clever, Joe, and the idea has much to commend it, but it changes nothing. I cannot stay here."

Joe admitted defeat. "All right. Let's go out the back way and follow the path round to the car park. That way we'll spare your blushes."

Ten minutes later Joe's ageing Vauxhall reversed into a parking space behind the chalet, and he retrieved their small amount of luggage and dragged it in through the tiny kitchen.

"I guessed Sheila wouldn't buy into this," Brenda said as she switched on the kettle, opened the cold box and took out teabags, milk and sugar. "In fact, as I said, I'm surprised you didn't go with her."

"Don't think I didn't think about it, but we all know the score on this kind of job. We need to be here, on site, just in case something happens." Holding the handles of both suitcases, he said, "I suppose you're having the double bedroom, and I'll have to settle for the twin. At least, that's how it was in Cornwall."

Brenda chuckled. "Yes, but I wasn't talking to you in Cornwall." She sidled up to him. "How about we share the double? I mean, it can get quite chilly in Lincolnshire, especially on a summer's night."

Joe tutted. "Feeling frisky already? We didn't come here for a weekend of fornication, Brenda. We have a job to do."

"True, but we don't need to be on the job all the time... Well, not that kind of job anyway."

This time he sighed. "All right. I'll put both cases in the double room."

By the time he returned from the bedroom, Brenda had made tea, and taking his cup, Joe stood at the front window, staring out at the loungers around the pool. "There's a familiar face."

Brenda joined him, looked out, and laughed. "I don't know who you're talking about Joe, but if it's this one nearest to us, you can't see her face."

The woman in question was the same one Edström had pointed out while showing them to their chalet. Then, she had been carrying a soft drink to her lounger. Now, she lay on the lounger in all her naked glory, her back to their window.

"Dr Delia Coll," Joe said, recalling his check of the files.

"My eye. It's Carol Liddle." He faced Brenda. "Remember her from Blackpool? Scum reporter for the West Yorkshire Chronicle."

He knew that Brenda would never be able to resist the inevitable jibes. "Ooh, Joe. I know we were kidding about the way you were supposed to have slept with her, but I didn't realise you and she got that close."

He tutted. "I caught a glimpse of her face when Edström was showing us to the chalet and pointed her out, and I checked the files before we gave them to Sheila. I recognised her right away. Now what is she doing swanning around in the altogether at a naturist resort?"

"Maybe she is a naturist, Joe."

"Yeah, maybe and I'm considering turning The Lazy Luncheonette into a topless restaurant, but I'm worried that it might put the draymen off their breakfast. Talk sense, Brenda. She's here under a false handle."

"How do you know?"

"You know your trouble? All this bare flesh is putting your thought processes and your hearing on hold. According to the files and Edström, her name is Delia Coll and she's a GP from Morley. So tell me again, why would Carol Liddle be taking a holiday here under a false name if not for a story?"

Brenda's response was a little more serious. "Maybe she's chasing the same thieves as us."

"And maybe I really will turn The Lazy Luncheonette into a topless caff. She's scum, Brenda. She's looking for the low-down on what the nuddies get up to, bed-hopping, wife swapping, that kind of thing."

"It doesn't happen, Joe... Well, maybe it does, but no more so than in any other holiday park. You heard Edström; naturism is not about sex."

"And I believe him, but would she? Liddle, I mean? Look at what she did in Blackpool. Had us bang to rights when we hadn't done anything. With her sort, the truth doesn't always matter. As long as she can invent a story for that rag."

Joe returned to the table and Brenda sat opposite him. "Maybe she's after you again," Brenda suggested.

"Daft. Who knows we're here?"

"Only half of Sanford. The half you've told. And if Ian Lofthouse at the Gazette has got the whisper, he could have passed it on to the Chron." She laughed. "I can see the headlines now: Sanford private eye and his doll in nudie seaside romps."

Joe laughed too. "You're as potty as Liddle. Oh, and that reminds me. Don't you think it's time you came clean?"

"Me? What have I done?"

"You knew about this place before we ever got here, didn't you? Being a naturist resort, I mean."

Brenda's face remained a picture of innocence. "How could I? And if I did, don't you think I would have warned you in advance?"

"You had your own agenda. Come on, Brenda, this is me you're talking to, not Sheila." A light bulb lit in his head. "You and George Robson joking in the Miners Arms last night. You were talking about this place weren't you, and he told you."

She gave way with a loud cackle. "All right, so yes, we were and he told me. You were blabbing it all over the pub about how you'd been hired to investigate thefts at this place and George Robson tipped me the wink. Apparently he and Owen were here on a fishing weekend earlier in the year. There's a fish farm not far from here, so he says. They were going to suss this place out for a lively night. You know what they're like for trapping off. But the minute they saw the sign, they backed out." She laughed. "Thank the lord for small mercies, eh? Can you imagine those two trolling about in their birthday suit?"

Joe suppressed a shudder at the imagery. "Why didn't you say something?"

"Two reasons. One, you were hyped over landing the job, and two, I fancied having a look around."

Joe was surprised. "You're not a naturist. You even told Edström that you don't share his convictions."

"No, but I have tried it."

This time Joe gaped. "You've what? When?"

"Years ago. Me and Colin. Before he died, obviously. We

saw this advert for a place in the Yorkshire Dales. Clothing optional, like this one, so we spent a weekend there. Colin was just embarrassed. Never took his shorts off. I stripped completely for a little while. Well, you know me, I've never been shy. But I wasn't totally at ease, Joe. I felt as if other people were staring at me, even though I knew they weren't. What I do remember was how comfortable I felt while I was naked, and I'm talking comfortable as in unrestricted, not easy as in the sense of being with others. Freedom like no knicker elastic getting caught in my leg, no bra straps trying to throttle me. And when George told me about this place, I thought I'd keep schtum and see what happened, especially after you and Sheila never bothered to check it out."

Still amazed, Joe shook his head. "Well, I'm stunned. You never cease to surprise me."

Brenda laughed again. "Maybe we could bring the 3rd Age Club here."

Joe found the suggestion just as funny. "Can you imagine what would happen if we put it forward at a meeting? There'd be a riot."

"And Sheila would be leading the revolutionaries." Her smile turned to a frown. "Trouble is, Joe, she's my bestie, and I miss having her with us."

"You must have had an idea. In fact, you said exactly that a few minutes ago. Just before she left."

"That doesn't alter how I feel about her not being here." Brenda drained her cup. "Now, come on. How about you change into your Speedos, I'll put my cozzy on and we can take a tour of the place, before this meeting?"

"Speedos? Shorts, more like." Joe glanced through the front window again. "And we can start by getting to know why Carol scum hack Liddle is here... Oh. Have you got those names from the list?"

"Of course. There are only three incidents. Welsby and Simpson, the couple Edström mentioned, another couple, Kesteven and Ormond, and a single man named Pollitt."

"Then we'll need to speak to them after Edström's made the grand announcement."

Chapter Five

There were about a hundred people in the bar when Joe and Brenda entered, and to a man and woman, they wore nothing or as close to nothing as made no difference. Relieved to find the barmaid – Olga according to her nametag – wearing a clean white shirt and a neat, black bowtie, he ordered a glass of lager for himself and Campari and soda for Brenda, and they waited off to one side while Edström, stood before the members and called for their attention.

Both were aware of their self-consciousness, Joe wearing only a pair of bright orange shorts which had last seen the light of day when visiting his ex-wife in Playa de Las Américas, Tenerife, earlier in the year, Brenda clad in a two-piece, skirted swimming costume which had languished in her wardrobe since her last holiday abroad, a trip to Ibiza in April. Edström wore nothing and while addressing his audience, he betrayed no trace of self-consciousness.

"Acclimatisation," Brenda whispered to Joe. "It's all about expanding your comfort zones."

"I think I left mine in Sanford," Joe muttered.

Edström opened the meeting. "Good afternoon, ladies and gentlemen, and please accept my apologies for disturbing your holiday, but we have a serious issue here at Sun Kissed. As you are aware, there have been a series of thefts on the site over the last three months. Since the police cannot allocate manpower to tracking down the thief or thieves, I have had no choice but to call in a team of specialist private investigators to look into the matter. They will need to speak to you individually, especially those members who have suffered thefts over the last few days. These people do not share our lifestyle preference, and at their request, I have to ask you to wear a robe or something similar when meeting with them."

A murmur of discontent ran through the audience. Joe, a veteran of many such meetings of the Sanford 3rd Age Club, recognised it, and was about to speak up, but before he could move forward, one of the members, a middle-aged man, getting short of hair, beat him to it.

"Surely they should accept our way of life, Mr Edström, and as such be ready to meet us on our terms, not theirs."

Joe stepped forward "Mr Chair—"

Edström chuckled. "I'm the proprietor, Joe, not the Chairperson." He faced the audience again. "Allow me to introduce the main investigator, Mr Joseph Murray." He gestured for Joe to come forward.

The number of times he had stood before an audience and made such an address, Joe should have felt at ease, but in this situation, it was impossible. Eventually, he focused his eyes on the windows gazing out over the pool, just above the head of the man who had come up with the objection.

"Can I ask you a question Mr…"

"Welsby. William Welsby."

"You've suffered a theft this week, Mr Welsby, haven't you?"

"Yes. An expensive Breitling wristwatch and my partner's purse were stolen."

"Then let me ask you this. If you were meeting with, say, your solicitor, even here on Sun Kissed, would you dress?"

"It wouldn't be likely to happen. I don't live in Skegness. I don't even live in Lincolnshire."

"And you're avoiding the question, sir." It grated on Joe to address the man as 'sir'. "No matter where you were meeting your lawyer, even here, you would dress. My partners, Mrs Jump and Mrs Riley, and I do not criticise your lifestyle choices, but we don't share them, and all we are asking is that you respect our choices just for the short while it will take to speak to you. If that's asking too much, then you can kiss goodbye to your Breitling wristwatch."

The manner in which he put the point, caused another

murmur of consternation, and Brenda stepped in. Unlike Joe, she had no problem focussing on the people rather than the background.

"Ladies and gentlemen, you'll have to forgive my colleague's brusque response. I work with him, and he creates no end of problems in that way. On the other hand, I can assure you that when it comes to this kind of problem, we are the best. I don't claim that we will get your property returned, but I do insist that we will track down and identify the thieves. All we ask in return, is that for the few minutes that we will be speaking to you, you put on some kind of clothing."

Welsby was not yet finished. "All right, but I have to say your friend looks a little short to be a police officer."

"I could say the same about you," Joe retorted while staring directly at Welsby's midriff. "But I haven't looked that closely at what you have to offer."

A rebellious rumble ran round the room and Brenda tutted. "Good old Joe. Jump in feet first and start a riot." To the members, she said, "Please forgive Mr Murray's insensitivity, ladies and gentlemen. He's a skilled detective, but he has a problem keeping his gob shut at times."

At the rear of the room, another man, and around the same age as Welsby, got to his feet. "You guarantee that you'll catch this thief, madam?"

The question took the heat out of the moment, but it also threw Brenda.

"I don't know about catch, Mr…"

"Pollitt. Trevor Pollitt. My chalet was broken into, and I lost an expensive mobile phone and a digital camera."

"You brought a camera to a holiday park where you're not allowed to use it?" Joe demanded.

"For when I visit Skegness and other areas."

Joe would have argued further, but Brenda stepped in again. "I'm sorry to hear this, Mr Pollitt, but just to correct you, I didn't say we would catch the thief, but I do say that we will identify him or her."

Edström stood front and centre again. "Ladies and gentlemen, we can toss this debate backwards and forwards all afternoon, and I'm sure you would all prefer to be out in the sunshine. As you all know, Margot and I are dedicated to nature, but in meetings with Mr Murray and his colleagues, we have had to take a step back and put on robes. And that is all we are asking of you."

The audience appeared to accept it this time, and Joe took out his list.

"There are several people we need to speak to. Mr Welsby and partner, Ms Simpson, Mr Kesteven and Ms Ormond, you, Mr Pollitt, and Dr Delia Coll. Mr Edström will find somewhere where we can meet in private, and we'll call for you as we need to speak to you. Does anyone have any questions?"

Towards the rear of the room, an elderly woman got to her feet. "Forgive me. Vivienne Foulkes, one of Mr Edström's oldest members. Do you have any power of arrest, Mr Murray?"

Joe chuckled. "I think you've been watching too many cops and robbers shows on TV, Mrs Foulkes. No, we do not have any power of arrest, but in the event that we can identify the thief – or thieves – we, along with Mr Edström and his wife, will hold them here until the police arrive."

With a satisfied nod, Vivienne Foulkes sat down, Joe and Brenda retired to the bar area, and Edström brought the meeting to a close.

As the members began to file out, the proprietor joined Joe and Brenda. "Why do you need to speak to Dr Coll?"

"I think we know her," Joe said, thinking on his feet. "I'm sure she's from our area."

"Ah. It's a social meeting?"

Brenda nodded. "Strictly speaking, yes, I suppose it is, but people like her, doctors, are usually pretty keen at noticing things. You never know what she may be able to tell us."

"Trust us, Håkan, we know what we're doing," Joe assured him. "Now where can we meet these people?"

"Chalet number one is free. I'll get you the key, and you can speak to them there, unless you prefer to interview them in your chalet."

Brenda agreed with the latter comment. "That would make sense, Joe. Invite them into our shed, and we can give them a cup of tea or whatever."

"That's gonna cost a fortune in teabags."

Brenda tutted. "You really are a born tightwad, aren't you?"

"Fully licensed and thoroughly professional."

"I'll leave you to it then," Edström said and left them.

As he wandered off, Carol Liddle came to them. "Daahlings, how absolutely gorgeous to see you," she squealed in a fake, upper class accent loud enough to be heard all over the room. "And you looked so healthy, Joe?"

She signalled the barmaid, and asked for a Bacardi and coke, and while she waited for it, she leaned forward and aimed a couple of air kisses at him, one on each cheek, and as she did so, she whispered, "I'm Delia Coll, a doctor. Got that? One word of my real name, and I'll crucify you and this cow in next Sunday's issue."

Joe played the part well, turning his eyes from her breasts when they dangled perilously close to his chest. "Good to see you, Delia. It's been a while, and the last time we met, you were wearing fancier duds than you are now."

"And I have to say, I never realised you two were sun worshippers as well as private eyes," Carol replied in her loud, fake voice.

"Did you listen to anything we said?" Brenda asked. "We're still trying to shake off our inhibitions to deal with these people."

"You should try it, daahling. Just let it all hang out." Carol lowered her voice again. "And you look as if you have plenty to hang out."

Brenda maintained a fixed smile, kept her lips tight and poured acid into her voice. "One more snide remark like that and you'll need to get dressed to cover the bruises."

Joe, too kept his voice down. "Tell you what, Delia, we really do need to speak to you, so why not come over to our chalet and we can have a cuppa and a long chat? We're in number seventeen."

"Gorgeous, old chum." Now Carol lowered her voice again. "And I do mean old. Ten minutes. Right?"

"Fine, oh, and while you're at it, put some clothes on. Seeing you like that is enough to put me off chicken for life."

Carol left and Joe and Brenda went into a soft conversation.

"Round one to us?" Brenda asked.

"Score draw, I think." Joe gulped down more lager. "We'll have to come to an arrangement with her. She doesn't want everyone to know who she is, and we don't want everyone to know the ins and outs of our investigation, so we'll have to call truce and negotiate a deal."

"As long as I get to send her to the dentist when we're through."

In the act of taking another drink, Joe paused. "Dentist?"

"Many more catty remarks and I'll kick her bloody teeth in."

He laughed. "I love it when you get all macho."

"I thought it was men who get macho."

"All right then, I love it when you go all amazon."

After finishing their drinks, they ambled back to the chalet, and once inside, Joe suggested, "Better put the kettle on. We might not like the silly mare, but we should make an effort to remain civilised."

Brenda clucked. "Damn. It's all right making her a cup of tea, Joe, but I completely forgot to pack the arsenic."

Carol arrived five minutes later, and maintaining the same fake air of good cheer, Joe greeted her warmly, ushered her into the chalet, closed the door and pointed to the table. The smile wiped from his face the moment he shut the door. "Sit you down and be ready to talk, I'll just repeat what I said in the bar, you start getting the knives out, and I'll make sure everyone here knows just who and what you are."

"Back at you," Carol retorted and joined Brenda at the table. "One word out of place and I'll bust you wide open in next Sunday's edition."

The reporter was wearing a thin, barely concealing wrap, and Joe purposely averted his eyes when he sat alongside

Brenda. He was about to make his opening gambit, when Carol spoke first.

"What are you two doing here? All right, so you said you're looking into these thefts, what possessed Edström to hire a couple of clowns like you?"

Joe replied, "Edström never told us the place was a naturist site, but as it happens, I have friends on the local police force. I've a question for you, but I'm willing to bet you won't answer us. Your turn."

"I've a big story coming down. And I mean big. This is for the West Yorkshire Chronicle but it'll go a lot further than that. If I can get to it, if I can get the evidence I need, this will go to the national Sundays. What I don't need are goons like you screwing the job up for me."

Brenda glared daggers of ice. "From all I can remember, the only one screwing anything up in Blackpool was you. What have you got against the truth?"

"It doesn't sell newspapers."

"And that validates the lies you tell, does it?"

Carol took a sip of tea, grimaced, and then laughed. "Who tells lies? I simply dress truth up in a more attractive manner. I mean, look at you two. A couple of hick private eyes from Sanford, turning up at a place like this and poking your noses into the thieving that's going on here. What kind of story is that? Much more fun if I write about your nosy-posy efforts and the jiggery-pokery you get up to while bouncing around wearing no more than what mother nature gave you."

Joe sensed that Brenda was on the point of losing her temper, but he maintained his equilibrium. "And how much further do you think you'll get with your story when we tell Edström who and what you really are? Now come on, Liddle. We need to strike a deal here. I'm not angling to put you on my Christmas card list. I wouldn't waste the ink and paper, not to mention the stamp considering the price of postage these days, but it's in our best interests to keep our mouths shut about you, provided you're willing to pass on any information that comes your way. And let's start by asking, who are you chasing and what has he done?"

"No names, no pack drill, and how do you know it's a he?" Carol's objection met with blank, bland stares. "All right, so I'm not interested in the resident tea leaf, so there's no competition, and if I do learn anything, I'll pass it on, and if you do identify the scroat or scroats, I can arrange for the Chronicle to pay you for the story."

"We'll bear it in mind," Joe said. "So go on. You're not trying to compete with us, so what are you doing?"

"Like I said, no names, no pack drill, but the implications are horrendous for our present, beloved administration. We're not exactly talking Cabinet minister, but the person concerned is married with a family, and comes here three or four times a year, hangs around baring all."

Joe gave a dismissive twitch of the head. "So you've got a politician who's also a naturist. It's a free country. It's not like he's committing treason."

"Quite right, and I believe the person concerned does have a reputation in Westminster for his—" Carol put on a broad, sly grin. "— or her naturist convictions. What Westminster, the cabinet, and the Prime Minister don't know is that this most happily married right honourable gentleman – or lady – turns up here with his, or her, bit on the side. What's worse, it's not always the same bit on the side. It changes. Sometimes it's fair-haired, sometimes it's dark, sometimes it's a bloodnut – a redhead. What's more, the distinguished member's bedhopping isn't confined to the Sun Kissed Holiday Park. He or she regularly visits other naturist camps in other parts of the country."

"But you just said that he's a naturist by conviction."

"That's right, Mrs Jump, but what if that conviction is a convenient excuse for weekends or full weeks of unadulterated fornication? You see, these nudist colonies—"

"Naturist parks," Brenda interrupted.

"Whatever you want to call them. These places have a fantastic advantage over your common or garden hotel. Absolute privacy. The press can't get anywhere near them. We'd never get closer than a thousand yards to get a photograph."

"Unless of course that member of the press happens to be a superduper, investigative reporter, prepared to throw off all her morals – such as they are – and her clobber for the sake of the story," Joe said.

"Spot-on, Joe Murray. So I have to hang around in the buff for a few days. Unlike your girlfriend here, what I have to show off isn't bad, and I have a threshold of embarrassment so high you couldn't reach that far."

Joe ignored the jibes. "Okay. Let's deal. Tell us who it is you're looking at, and if we get any hint of shenanigans, we'll pass the message on. By return, if you get any clue as to who's behind these thefts, you give us the tip off."

Carol shook her head. "No deal." She hastened on before Joe and Brenda could argue. "It's not that I don't trust you. I'm certain you won't go shouting your mouth off, but this is a potential gold mine for me, and if you get tanked up and let slip one word, even by accident, you'll lose me a lot of money. My best offer is as I've already said. If I come across anything, I'll pass it on to you two, and in return you keep your mouth shut about me. Deal?"

Joe looked at Brenda, she looked at him, and they nodded.

Chapter Six

With three sets of people, two couples and one single man, yet to interview, Joe calculated that they would be finished by half past four. He didn't anticipate the arguments to come, many of them irrelevant to the thefts.

He took them alphabetically by surname on the relevant booking, which brought Neil Kesteven and Gina Ormond to their chalet first.

Kesteven appeared to be in his late forties, a distinguished head of dark hair (Brenda would later swear that he used Grecian 2000) topped a lean, tanned face, with soft, brown eyes which belied his irritation. He spoke with a classless English accent, which could have placed him anywhere in the country, but from his membership file, they learned that he was from Bristol.

Gina Ormond, his partner, was a good deal younger. According to her file, she was only just turned thirty years of age, and to their surprise, she was American. A fit and athletic woman with strong arms and hands, the kind Joe in his infinite lack of wisdom, would normally associate with a man. She spoke with an undisguised accent, which Joe, once again biased by his lack of experience, placed somewhere around New York. This time, however, he was not wrong. She was a native of Brooklyn.

Both wore towelling bathrobes, and it was obvious that they were too hot. Even if it were not obvious, Kesteven wasted no time in telling them.

"I've never been subjected to these rules in all the times I've visited naturist parks."

Joe remained blunt and unrepentant. "Then we're both like fish out of water, Mr Kesteven. We've never had to work on a naturist park before, and it's just as uncomfortable for us as it is for you."

"You know, you couldn't do this in the States," Gina said. "I'd have had my attorney nailing you to a cross."

"It's no different in this country, Ms Ormond. You don't have to speak to us, but you've been robbed. I don't say we can get your missing items back, but we can see the perpetrators brought to justice." Joe paused to drive home his point. "Only if you're willing to talk to us."

Gina shrugged and fell silent, ready to leave the debate to her partner.

Brenda delivered tea, and sat with Joe, facing the couple. "Just as an aside, how come you two are together? Please don't misunderstand me, but you're a few years older than Ms Ormond, and you're British, Mr Kesteven."

It was Gina who answered. "I met Neil in America. He invited me over here, I came to this country, and we fell in love. There's no big mystery, Mrs Jump."

"Forgive me. I was only being nosy."

Joe spoke up in support of his companion. "We find it helps in our game."

Kesteven waded in. "According to Dr Coll, your game is feeding lorry drivers, Mr Murray. You ran a café or something somewhere up near York."

"Closer to Leeds, as it happens, and she's right, but I double up as a private investigator, and trust me, I'm one of the best. It helps make money when I lose it feeding bolshie truckers. Now can we stick to the point?"

Kesteven conceded with a shrug. "What is it you want to know?"

"First, what did you lose in the burglary?"

"An expensive laptop. A MacBook. I store a lot of data on it, much of it related to my students. I'm a lecturer in politics and economics, at the University of Bristol. If – when – whoever stole that machine manages to hack through the passwords, he can make a small fortune selling on my students' details, not to mention other works stored on there: papers prepared for publication, the manuscript of a forthcoming book. You understand the kind of thing I mean?"

Kesteven paused his final question with a look which said he doubted Joe's ability to comprehend one word in ten.

"Do us both a favour, Mr Kesteven, and don't talk down to me, or I'll try to blind you with food technology." He glowered. "That's cooking, to you."

Once more, Kesteven shrugged. "Well, now you know what was taken. Is there anything else?"

"Just a couple more questions. Which night was this?"

"Tuesday," Gina replied. "Sometime between seven o'clock and ten o'clock."

"You're certain of the time?"

"We left the chalet at seven to go for dinner," Kesteven said. "Before you ask, yes, we locked up. After dinner, we stayed in the bar chatting with Ignatius Isherwood."

"A senile, sex obsessed old boy," Gina put in. "He's well known here and everyone calls him Aye-Aye."

Joe agreed. "We haven't met him yet. And you went back to the chalet at ten? Is that right?"

"Yes. When we got there, the door was unlocked but it hadn't been forced. Whoever got in must have had a key. We checked and my MacBook had gone, along with the few pounds in loose change which Gina left lying around on top of the fireplace."

Brenda had confined herself to making notes, but now asked, "You reported the matter to Mr Edström. Did you contact the police or your insurers?"

"We left it to Mr Edström to deal with the police, and as of right now, I haven't yet contacted my insurers, but I did get in touch with the university, and advised them to upgrade all their passwords."

Joe put the final question. "Have you been out of the park? You know, checking the local secondhand shops in Skegness?"

"No."

"You're not that keen to get your gear back?"

"That's not the case at all, Mr Murray. According to the best estimates of our IT department, anyone trying to hack the machine would take several days to break through the passwords, and then he or she would have to download the information for it to be of any use."

Joe smiled. "Okay. That's fine. We have all the information we need. Let me just repeat, I can't make any promises, but if we do turn up anything regarding your machine, we'll let you know. Could you ask Mr Pollitt to come and see us, please?"

The couple left, and Brenda wiped imaginary sweat from her brow. "He was a cantankerous sod, wasn't he? He reminded me of you when you've got a paddy on you."

"I love the way you boost my self-esteem, Brenda."

Trevor Pollitt was not much of an improvement. He entered their chalet wearing a pair of swimming trunks, sat opposite them, declined tea, and protested his dissatisfaction with a) having to put on the small garment, and b) having to run through the burglary for the third time.

"Once to Edström, once to my solicitor, and now to you."

"All we need to know, Mr Pollitt, is what went missing and when," Joe assured him.

He pointed a finger at Brenda. "I told her in the bar. My laptop. Gone. And it can cost me a bloody fortune."

Brenda frowned. "How so?"

"I run my own IT company. There's tons of information on that machine: plans for games, plans for other apps, marketing plans, even my accounts. Whoever nicked it could make a small fortune, and the worst of it is, if he gets to sell the games off, and I rebuild, he'll claim the bloody copyright."

"Which was presumably why you had to contact your solicitor?" Joe asked.

"Correct. I have backups at home, naturally. My biggest worry is him checking out my accounts."

Joe and Brenda exchanged suspicious glances, and Pollitt picked up on it.

"Oh, come on. You're business people, you know what it's like. You don't declare every single penny that comes in."

"You're wrong, Mr Pollitt," Joe told him. "I run a highly

profitable business, and I do declare every penny that comes in and goes out. Anyway, let's not get sidetracked. When did this burglary take place?"

"Tuesday night."

Joe and Brenda were surprised. "The same night as Kesteven and Ormond were burgled?"

"He was obviously very busy that night," Pollitt sneered. "Yes, and as I understand it from Kesteven, the thieves stole his laptop, too."

"Do you have any idea of the time of the break-in?"

Pollitt looked around the room, accessing his memory, Joe guessed. "I went out about half past seven for dinner. After dinner, I went back to the chalet and everything was fine. Then about ten o'clock, maybe a little after, I decided on a nightcap, and made my way back to the bar. I got back to the chalet just before midnight and the door was open."

"And, of course, since then, you haven't heard a thing. Have you checked out the local seccondhand shops?"

Pollitt shook his head. "You're not naturist, so you won't appreciate what I'm going to say. When I come to places such as Sun Kissed, I tend to stay within the confines of the park. I am a naturist by conviction. I dislike being encumbered, constrained by clothing." He swept his hands down his body from shoulder to knee.

"I'd hardly call those swimming trunks an encumbrance," Brenda commented, and Pollitt left with an agreement to send Welsby and Simpson along.

"I figure these two will be the worst," Joe said while Brenda switched on the kettle again. "If I'm right, he was tuning up for a scrap in the bar."

She smiled mock sweetly. "Don't worry, Joe. I'll protect you."

Joe was right. From the moment Welsby and his partner entered the chalet he was sultry, irritated, and his partner, a slender blonde somewhere in her early fifties, left the talking to him.

They had both put on thin robes, similar to the one Carol Liddle wore earlier, and the supposed infringement of his rights to be as nature intended, was eating away at Welsby.

"We come here for a reason, Murray. We're not accustomed to people insisting we fall into line with textiles."

Joe stood up to him. "And as my colleague said earlier, Mr Welsby, we're not accustomed to people trying to drag us out of our comfort zones. You have the same problem, Ms Simpson?"

She shrugged. "Frankly, yes. However, I'm not quite as forceful as my partner, and perhaps a little more willing to compromise."

Joe detected a slight accent in the way she pronounced 'willing'. It came out more like 'villing'. He checked Brenda's notes, and then smiled. "Curious accent for someone from Birmingham."

She returned his smile. "I'm British, but I spent many years working in the Netherlands, and I suppose the Dutch accent has infiltrated my natural Brummie."

"Yes, well, we can sit here arguing the toss between naturism and non-naturism, or we can get on with it. Let's get down to brass tacks?" Without waiting for a response, Joe pressed on. "You said you were missing an expensive Breitling wristwatch, Mr Welsby, and your partner's purse was stolen."

"Yes."

"In this kind of situation, money is almost impossible to recover, but can you tell me, Ms Simpson, roughly how much you had in your purse?"

She answered right away. "Only a few pounds. It's not the money which is important, Mr Murray. There were credit and debit cards, too. As I'm sure you're aware, anyone securing such cards can soon access the magnetic strip on the back, and before you know it, they're spending on my various accounts."

"You stopped the cards?" Brenda asked.

"Of course. I rang the bank right away, first thing Wednesday morning."

Joe frowned. "So you were burgled on Tuesday night?"

"That's correct," Wells reassured him. "Sometime between

seven and ten o'clock."

"The same timeframe as Kesteven and Ormond, and Trevor Pollitt."

Welsby agreed. "We compared notes with them the following morning."

"Okay. I won't ask if you checked out the secondhand shops, but would you recognise this wristwatch again?"

"On the face of it, no, but the back of the watch bears its serial number. You may not be aware, but Breitling are similar to Rolex. Every timepiece has its own serial number."

Joe nodded. "You didn't lose a laptop?"

"No. I don't bring one with me."

Joe thanked the couple and they left.

"One of them is telling porkies," he said to Brenda, "and while you're busy trying to work it out, I'll tell you. It's Pollitt."

She disappeared into the kitchen, and returned a few moments later with fresh tea. "How do you know?"

"When he stood up whingeing in the bar, he said he'd lost a mobile phone and a digital camera. Talking to us, he never mentioned either of them, and instead claims he's lost a pricey laptop. I'm not saying he wasn't burgled, but I think he's laying it on thick for his insurers."

***

A couple of miles away and an hour after leaving Sun Kissed, Sheila settled into a small, comfortable room of a B&B just off the seafront, and after making herself a cup of tea, began to go through the information Edström had given them.

She did not expect Joe or Brenda to understand her objections to places like Sun Kissed. They would assume that she was simply prudish to the degree of Victorian virginity, and her upright behaviour throughout her life might lead anyone to conclude the same. She was nothing of the kind. Like her best friend Brenda, she had enjoyed something of a love life since the death of her husband, but unlike Brenda, she had enjoyed it in absolute privacy. No one, not Brenda, not Joe, not her sons, absolutely no one knew anything of her gentlemen friends. Until Martin, that is, but he was impossible to keep secret for no other reason than they married (not that she recalled their brief months together with anything approaching fondness).

The truth was much simpler. She found nudity, whether herself or other people nearby, uncomfortable and embarrassing. Throughout their many adventures with the 3rd Age Club she and Brenda had shared a room, but where Brenda was without inhibition and had no hesitation in stripping off completely in the middle of their room, Sheila always retired to the bathroom to undress and dress. Underwear, fine, nakedness, never. When lazing around the fine, sandy beaches of the Mediterranean, where topless sunbathing was common and the public looked upon it with a blasé acceptance, Sheila would never remove the upper part of her bathing costume. Brenda did. But that was Brenda all over. In Sheila's case, the only men and women who had ever gazed upon her naked body were those of the medical profession and the few men with whom she entertained infrequent dalliances.

If such displays made her cringe with embarrassment, the prospect of staying at a holiday park where nudity was not frowned upon but encouraged, was beyond the pale, and she guessed that Brenda knew in advance that she, Sheila, would refuse to stay there. Even walking with Joe back to their cars, she had kept her eyes fixed straight ahead, diverting them to look away only when a young couple, both without clothing, crossed their path.

She would miss her friends' company. A sacrifice she had to make, albeit for only one night. Joe had promised that twenty-four hours hence they would all be in a hotel distanced from Sun Kissed, and he and Brenda could deal with the investigation at ground zero. Her voluntary separation did not mean, however, she could not contribute to their inquiries, and she was certain they would clear it up quickly, and allow themselves a few days in Skegness to enjoy the more convivial and (to her way of thinking) socially acceptable amenities the Lincolnshire coast had to offer.

But in the meantime, within the solitude of her tiny room, there was work to be done.

Edström's administration was of the highest order. His files listed all the members and spelled out all the necessary information: name, age, gender, home address, telephone number and email address and emergency contact should the need arise. Beyond that, the clerical records were minimal. Under additional information, members could list medical conditions and their personal preferences. There was little of such information on any of the records, the most striking of which was a woman named Diane Randleson. A curious woman who insisted that she would not be seen naked in public, and while she had no objections to nudity, she would wear a swimming costume at all times when she was outside.

It was an anomaly to Sheila's way of thinking. What was the point in joining a naturist community, if she was unwilling to take full part in that community?

She put the question to one side as she leafed through the membership files, and concentrated on the photographs.

The files before her revealed a membership of varied ages, gender, ethnicity, marital status and so on, and once again, Edström demonstrated that he left nothing to chance. Every member, short-term or otherwise, had to provide a head and shoulders photograph, or have such a photograph taken when they checked in for their holiday. She assumed, although she had no evidence to back her up, that members would be issued with an identity card and could be challenged by any member of staff.

It was while she was concentrating on the images that she came across a familiar and unwelcome face: Carol Liddle.

Memories of Blackpool the previous winter flooded her mind, and the scurrilous, underhanded means by which the woman secured her stories. It occurred to her right away that Joe and Brenda would not be aware of the reporter's presence, and she took out a mobile phone to ring Brenda. Then she stopped.

She did not care why Liddle was staying at Sun Kissed. It would be a story, no doubt, and a woman like her would not be averse to bugging the chalet or even hacking mobile phones. Was such a thing possible? There was no doubt that she would recognise Joe and Brenda. They had, after all, shown her up in Blackpool.

Sheila had no choice. She would have to swallow her discomfort, return to Sun Kissed and warn her friends.

Chapter Seven

It was almost five o'clock. Joe and Brenda were talking about their plans for an evening in the dining room, and ways and means by which they could monitor the staff and other guests.

Joe had already installed a miniature camera in a discreet corner of the chalet, part hidden by a china ornament, a cartoonlike casting of a Jack Russell dog named Wilf (according to the tag around its absurdly thin neck).

The camera was connected to his laptop by wi-fi, and he was hoping that he could pick up the signal from the dining room. The machine would alert him to any activity in their temporary dwelling.

"It cost me an arm and a leg," he said. "Over two hundred nicker for a camera small enough to fit inside a cigarette packet."

"The amount you make from your PI work, I'm sure you can afford it," Brenda said. She was about to say more when Sheila's Fiat turned into the small parking area behind the chalet. "Hey up, it's Mrs Prim and Prissy. What's she doing back here?"

"Maybe she fancies eyeing up some potential male?"

Brenda guffawed. "I dare you to say that to her."

"I…er…"

"Say what to me?" Sheila demanded as she marched into the chalet.

"Nothing, dear. We were talking about you not to you." Brenda left the table, moved to the kitchen and switched on the kettle. "Would you like a cup of tea?"

"I definitely need tea."

Joe came away from his camera, checked the view on his

laptop, was happy that it covered the main door and the entrance to the kitchen, and closed the lid of the machine, putting it sleep. "You must have something on your mind, Sheila?"

"Yes. Dr Delia Coll."

Joe laughed. "You mean Carol Liddle."

Sheila's gape betrayed her surprise, quickly buried by anger. "You mean you know? Why have I just driven from my bed-and-breakfast to this terrible place to warn you when you already knew? Couldn't you ring me?"

Brenda returned with three beakers of tea and spread them across the table. "We might ask the same question. Why didn't you just ring us?"

Sheila laid the buff folder on the table, and tapped it with an irritable finger. "I was afraid she might have recognised you and bugged this place or worse, she might be monitoring your phone calls. I don't know if that's possible, but with her, you never know, and if she's seen you, she's almost certainly —"

Brenda interrupted. "Seen us? She was here. Joe recognised her by the pool." She guffawed. "I was surprised. I mean, she didn't have stitch on but he still clocked her."

Joe scowled her into silence, and over a beaker of tea, he and Brenda went on to explain the exchange between themselves and Carol Liddle. When he was through, he asked, "How did you know?"

"Two things." Sheila leafed through the folder and took out Carol Liddle's membership form. "First and foremost, a photograph of her on her membership agreement. Second, you probably haven't noticed, but Dr Delia Coll is an anagram of Carol Liddle."

To confirm it, Joe took out a pad and pen, scribbled down Carol Liddle's name and then crossed the letters out as he translated the anagram. He conceded Sheila's point. "You're right. It is. And no, I didn't notice."

Brenda chuckled. "We noticed everything else about her. Literally. She was wearing nothing but her Ray Bans in the bar and while she was lazing by the pool, and when she came in here, she was only wearing a semi-transparent wrap. To be fair, she's not in bad nick for a scumbag, and," she jerked a thumb at Joe, "he got a proper eyeful."

Joe let out a fake yawn. "Seen it all before, and better organised."

This time it was Brenda who put on a mock face of modesty. "Thank you, Joe. Nice of you to say so."

Sheila's irritation increased by the minute. "You two really do get on my nerves. Do you know how difficult it was for me to come back here?"

"Take it easy, Sheila," Joe said. "While you are here, why don't you hide in the chalet for a couple of hours, and then join us for dinner?"

"With all these naked people about? I don't think so."

"They dress for dinner," Brenda insisted. "Edström told us if you remember. You won't see anything you're not meant to see." She took her best friend's hand. "Come on, Sheila. It won't be the same without you. How am I supposed to wind Joe up if you're not there to help?"

In view of their persistence, Sheila took a step back, but not all the way. "Very well. I'll have dinner with you, but I won't be drinking. I'll have to drive back to my digs after dinner because I will not spend one night in this place."

"That's more like it."

"The standard triumvirate," Brenda declared.

Joe frowned. "It's unusual you using long words like that, Brenda."

"What? Triumvirate?"

"No. Standard."

Brenda laughed it off, and Sheila smiled at Joe's good-natured dig.

For the next hour, Joe and Brenda took turns at people watching through the chalet window, identifying as many members as they could from the head and shoulder photographs in Edström's files. In deference to her deep-seated objections, they allowed Sheila to keep herself to the back of the room, working between her iPad and Joe's laptop, seeking any background that might be available on those members.

"This could be interpreted as spying, you know," Brenda said.

"It is spying," Joe declared. "We need to know who they are, who we're dealing with."

"And don't forget we need to look at the staff," Sheila commented from the back of the room.

"Why do you think I asked Edström for his employees' files?" Joe said. "If these thefts have been spread over the last ten or eleven weeks, as Edström insists, it's less likely to be one of the guests unless we can tie any of them down to the dates of the thefts."

"I've already done that," Sheila said, "and there's only one member who fits the bill. Diane Randleson. She's been here any number of times over the last thirteen weeks, mostly for weekends, but occasionally like now, for longer."

Brenda had already identified her. "A tall, leggy blonde. Odd thing, though. I've seen her walk past a couple of times, on the way to the bar, and she's not in the altogether. She wears a bikini."

Again it was Sheila who brought them up to speed. "She refuses to be seen nude in public . It doesn't make much sense to me, I must admit. I mean, what is the point of turning up at a place like this, where nudity is – let's be honest about it – expected, and then refusing to take part?"

"We're refusing," Joe pointed out.

"Yes, Joe, but we're not members. We're working here. If you check the file, she's signed up for full membership."

Brenda came down on the side of the park. "Edström did say that the place is clothing optional. You have to tolerate nudity, not necessarily join in."

Sheila was not convinced. "I accept that, but with the best will in the world, Edström and his wife need long-term members to have any chance of making the park pay its way, and they're like any other zealots. They may permit you to wander around in swimsuits or underwear, but in reality, they'd like to see you lose the theoretical shackles of convention. And I'm beginning to wish I'd never come back. I should have connected with Zoom and spoke to you over the video link."

"Oh don't be so prissy."

Sheila reacted to her friend's disparaging remark. "We're not all like you, Brenda. Some of us believe in established principles, and one of those principles is cover thyself up."

Joe murmured muted agreement, and Brenda turned on them both.

"You know what your trouble is, don't you? It's exactly as Edström pointed out. You're linking naturism with sex, and it has nothing to do with it." She waved an irritated arm at the window. "For all you know, these people might have sex once a year on their wedding anniversary, or maybe once every ten years, when the urge takes them. They're naturists not raving rompers. The two things don't go together other than in your minds."

Joe tried to suppress a smile. "In that case, will we see you parading in the altogether tomorrow?"

"No. It'll probably be too cold." And with that tongue-in-cheek remark, Brenda brought the acerbic debate to an end.

A little over an hour later, with the time coming up to seven o'clock, Sheila secured her iPad in her car, Joe tucked his laptop in its bag and left it in the bedroom, and with all three suitably dressed, they stepped out of the chalet, ignored the few people still taking in the ultraviolet, and made their way across to the bar/dining room, where they were invited to choose a table, and study the menu.

"Another three converts?" the elderly man on the next table asked.

"No. We're the private eyes and we're still feeling our way round," Joe said, and Brenda dissolved into helpless giggling. "What? What have I said?"

"It's not what you said, Joe it's the way you phrased it. Naturist site. Feeling our way round."

"And who is that said we're obsessed with S-E-X?"

The old man spoke up. "Ignatius Isherwood," he introduced himself. "Most people call me Aye-Aye."

"Joe Murray. And these are my two friends, Brenda Jump and Sheila Riley."

Isherwood's eyes almost popped. "Good Lord. A ménage à

trois?"

Brenda laughed again, Joe snorted, but Sheila took umbrage. "We are nothing of the kind. We're simply good friends and workmates."

"My apologies, dear lady. That being the case, what are my chances?"

The waiter appeared as Aye-Aye asked the question, and advised them, "Take no notice of the silly old sod. Lost his wife a couple of years ago, and he's been looking for a quick bunk up ever since. He's harmless enough. Just a bit potty. I'm Ellis, your waiter. Are you ready to order?"

"Give us a few minutes, son," Joe suggested. The waiter wandered off and Joe cast a pointed glance at Brenda. "I'll ask again. What were you saying about how naturism isn't about sex?"

"You heard the lad. The old boy's doolally. Anyway, forget him. What are having?"

"I think I'll have the baked haddock," Sheila said, and Joe concurred while Brenda opted for a chicken salad, and while Sheila asked for still water and Brenda ordered a glass of house white, Joe chose a glass of lager.

"When the waiter delivers the food," he said, "I'm going to try something. Just back me up by saying you left it in the chalet."

Sheila frowned. "Left what in the chalet?"

"His sanity probably," Brenda commented. "Or his Y-fronts."

"Grow up, both of you. The waiter's staff, isn't he? He was working behind the bar earlier, too. Great job for earwigging, and didn't we say a member of staff might be favourite? Just follow my prompt."

When their food arrived, they noted his name: Ellis Allyn, and as he delivered the plates, Joe said, "Brenda, where's my camera?"

"You left it in the chalet."

Joe put on a frown. "You were supposed to pick it up."

"I thought you were."

He leaned back to let the young waiter place the plate in

61

front of him. "Sorry, sport. You can't get the staff, you know."

"You're preaching to the choir, sir. Enjoy, all of you, and if you're posting reviews to Tripadvisor, don't forget my name's Ellis."

"Count on it," Joe agreed.

Ellis went away and Sheila frowned at Joe. "Having told everyone we're private investigators, do you really think that idiotic idea will work?"

"It's worth a punt."

While they ate, Brenda brought up the obvious. In a voice not much louder than a whisper, she asked, "Is your little spy camera working, Joe?"

"It is. But my proper camera is in my pocket." He patted the sides of his gilet. "If anyone goes looking for it, they'll come away empty-handed."

"But we'll have our man and we can be away from this disgusting place," Sheila said.

Her two friends let the remark pass, and Brenda opened up a friendly discussion on the places they had visited in the past, with or without other members of the Sanford 3rd Age Club. Joe contributed occasionally, but his concentration was on the Sun Kissed members as they arrived for the evening meal. Accessing his near-eidetic memory, recalling their afternoon's work and his brief reading of the files, he noted that Isherwood was joined by Arabella Simpson and Bill Welsby. There were other cliques to which he could not put names, but he was intrigued to find Carol Liddle, who had been there for almost three-quarters of an hour, joined by Diane Randleson at about seven-thirty, but at the same time, Diane's friend, Renata Chappell, was noticeable by her absence.

Logic told him that either Randleson or Chappell was the target of Ms Liddle's insidious brand of journalism and he made a decision to make a more intensive check on the two women. For the time being, he smiled ruefully to himself. Undercover? Carol Liddle was as transparent as the robe she had worn when she visited him and Brenda earlier in the afternoon.

The meal over, some people, amongst them Isherwood's dinner companions, and Neil Kesteven and Gina Ormond, left the dining room while other members were settling down for an evening of drinks and convivial conversation, Edström making occasional rounds, ensuring everyone was content, well-catered for, and Joe, alert for every move of every person in the room, reassuring the proprietor that everything was as it should be.

With time coming up to nine fifteen, Edström was absent once again, the rhubarb hum of conversation was disturbed by an ear-piercing scream, and a moment later, an agitated Margot came hurrying in, and made for Carol Liddle.

The proprietor's wife made no effort to keep her voice down. "Doctor Coll, I'm sorry to trouble you, but you must come quickly. It's Ms Chappell. I think she's been murdered."

Chapter Eight

Almost at once it occurred to Joe, Sheila and Brenda that the situation would blow Liddle's cover and their knowledge of her persuaded them that she would bite back by exposing their fictitious antics in the tabloids.

"You'd better go with them, Joe," Brenda said, but she was too late. He was already on his feet and crossing the room.

Caught in an inescapable quandary, Carol Liddle was floundering. "I, er, well, really, it's a job for … I mean, I'm here on holiday, and I…"

She tailed off as Joe arrived and smiled upon her. "Oh come on, Doctor. You'd better check on the victim before we call the police. Tell you what, I'll come with you." He beamed at Margot. "Dr Coll and I are old friends. Isn't that right, Delia?"

"Er, yes. Of course. Me and Joe go way back."

"Then come on. Let's check it out."

Her face a mixture of puzzlement and relief, Margot led them from the dining room, through the corridor and to the ladies' toilet where she pushed open the door and ushered them through, before following and closing the door behind her.

Renata Chappell lay naked and prone on the tiled floor beneath the hand basins, one blood-smeared hand clutching to her throat, where it had been sliced open.

"Just follow my lead," Joe muttered to Carol as they both bent over the woman.

He positioned himself between the body and Margot, so that she could not see him take Carol's hand and stretch it towards the body. Carol struggled slightly, refusing to touch

Renata, but Joe clung onto her hand while checking for a pulse with his right finger and thumb. "She's dead," he whispered. "You tell Margot."

"No. You."

"It'll look odd coming from a private eye rather than a doctor. Just do it."

They stood and straightened up. Still shaking, Carol faced Margot. "I'm sorry. She's snuffed it."

Joe frowned at the street vernacular and Margot chewed her fist.

"You need to get the police out, Margot," Joe told her.

"Yes, but—"

"It's vital," Joe said. "Isn't that right, Doctor?"

"Oh. Er, yes. I'm sorry, you have to call the filth... I mean the police."

Joe took the initiative once again. "And you can't let anyone into this room until they've been here and sussed it out. Even then, the CSI team will need to go through the place with a fine-toothed comb. It's likely this room will be closed for the next twenty-four, forty-eight hours."

Margot was appalled. "What will our lady members do?"

"A cork?" Carol suggested, and Joe scowled at her.

"Is that serious medical advice, Dr Coll?" he asked.

"I, er, sorry. I'm not... I'm just a little disturbed. You know. It's not every day you go on holiday and find a murder victim in the rest room."

"We need to get out and lock the door, Margot, and then call the cops. After that, I suggest you get your husband to make an announcement. If he doesn't want to do it, I will."

"Thank you, Mr Murray, Doctor."

They made their way out of the toilets and along the corridor. Margot diverted to the office where she would talk with her husband, and call the police, and Joe accompanied Carol back to the dining room.

"Come and sit with Sheila, Brenda, and me," he suggested. "We need to talk and it's best if we shut out earwigs."

"I'll just get my bag."

Several people waylaid Joe as he made his way back to the table, but he remained noncommittal, telling them that Edström would make an announcement soon. He had barely sat down, when Carol Liddle joined them, and they brought their heads together for what must have seemed like a council of war.

"You're in schtum," Joe told Carol. "Unless we handle this properly, You'll be shown up as a reporter. Offhand, I'd say you're hard pressed to avoid it, but we'll do what we can to keep you covered. Not that you deserve it, but I don't fancy having you slagging us off out of spite. First question: this Chappell woman. Was she the one you were looking into?"

Carol did not hesitate to answer. "No. Were you looking at her?"

"Not specifically. We've only just started and we're more interested in the staff. What about Chappell's girlfriend, the woman you were sat with? Diane Randleson or whatever her name is."

"Again, no. I'm not going to tell you who it is, but it's neither of those two, and if you're looking at the crew, my mark won't be on your radar either."

Sheila resorted to more practical questions. "Had she been dead long, Joe?"

He shook his head. "She was still warm. It's happened in the last half hour, hour at most, and that leaves us three – sorry, us four in the clear." He aimed a finger at Carol. "I've had my eye on you all evening, and you never left the table, and we three have been together since about five o'clock this afternoon so we can alibi each other."

Edström appeared again, his face grim, and called for order.

"Ladies and gentlemen, forgive me for interrupting your evening. There has been a serious incident in the ladies restroom. We have called the police, and they say we are not permitted to enter the room, and we should all stay here in the bar, until they arrive."

From across the floor, Vivienne Foulkes spoke up. "And what do we do if we need the ladies, Mr Edström?"

"We have staff facilities, Mrs Foulkes, and Margot and I will be on call all evening, to escort you. The police say that if any of us need to leave the room for such a reason, we should not be alone."

As the woman continued complaining, Sheila leaned into Joe. "Vivienne Foulkes. Fifty-four years old, widow, permanent member, visits three or four times a year."

"Yes. We know. She introduced herself earlier." Joe looked over Mrs Foulkes, or as much as he could see. Small, apparently overweight, and she had been knocking back glasses of spirit all evening. "Can't see her as a cat burglar," he said. He focused on Carol. "Is she your mark?"

"I've told you, Murray, I'm saying nothing, but for reference, she is not the one I'm interested in. Look, I'm grateful for you getting me out of the poop back there, but let's not pretend we're friends, huh?"

Diane Randleson spoke up. "I really must go back to the chalet and check on Renata. Do I need someone to come with me?"

Edström was nonplussed, and it was immediately obvious to Joe, that he and his wife did not know how to handle the news.

Joe got to his feet. "Excuse me, Håkan. I'm more familiar with this kind of thing than you. Would you like me to speak to the young lady?"

"That would be good of you, Mr Murray." Edström faced the woman. "Would you like to come with me to the general office, Ms Randleson?"

She put on a puzzled expression, but nevertheless accompanied Joe and Edström out of the bar, and along the corridor, to the main reception area where Edström showed her into the small office. While he took a seat behind the desk, Joe sat alongside the woman, and the manager pulled out a bottle and poured a small brandy which he placed on the desk in front of her.

"Will you deal with this, Mr Murray," Edström said.

"Diane… You don't mind if I call you Diane, do you?" Joe waited for her to give permission with a brief nod. "I'm afraid we have some bad news. Your friend, Renata, has been found dead in the ladies toilet."

As far as Joe could recall, it was only the second time he had had to make the announcement. The first time was in Inverness the previous year when he had to tell an entire film crew that one of their leading actresses had been murdered. Prepared for Ms Randleson's distress, he felt uncomfortable.

Her reaction surprised him. He'd expected tears, but there was nothing. Her hand shook, but aside from reaching out for the brandy and downing it in one gulp, that was it.

At length, she gathered herself together. "Is that why we're waiting for the police?"

"Yes. And just so you know, from all I can see, it was foul play. She was murdered."

Once again there was no significant reaction. Just another moment or two of silence. "You're an expert are you?"

The question rattled Joe, but he made an effort to suppress his irritation. "As you already know, I'm a private investigator and I have a reputation for solving murders. I've seen more than enough, and I know the signs. Renata's throat was cut open, and unless she was suicidal and determined to cause herself as much pain as possible, then someone else did the deed." It was a smart aleck answer, designed to drive home the obvious. "What can you tell us about her?"

"Very little. She's a friend. Not a close friend, just... I don't know. A pal."

Like so many other aspects of Sun Kissed Holiday Park, her answer was somewhere beyond the boundaries of what he would call normal. Why would anyone go on holiday, especially to a naturist site, with someone who wasn't a particularly close friend? The answer occurred to him right away but he lacked the temerity to suggest the obvious.

"The police will be here soon," Edström said, "and I'm sure they'll want to speak to you before anyone else, Ms Randleson."

"And I'm not sure what I can tell them. I only met her a couple of months ago, at another naturist park. We got on okay, and I've been a regular here for the last three months, as you know, Mr Edström, so I invited her along, and she said okay."

"No boyfriends hovering in the background?"

Diane looked uncomfortable with Joe's question. "Not that I know of."

Joe decided to test the waters. "Girlfriends then?"

It brought a withering stare from Diane. "She wasn't that way inclined, and before you ask, neither am I."

Joe held up his hand in surrender. "Sorry. Didn't mean to tread on your corns, but the police will ask the same question." He got to his feet. "I, er, I'm sorry for your loss. Can I leave Ms Randleson with you, Håkan?"

"Of course. And thank you, Joe."

Joe made his way back to the bar, rejoined his friends, to discover that Carol Liddle had moved on, and was now sitting with the old boy, Ignatius Isherwood.

"Our company not good enough for her?" he asked as he took his seat.

"We haven't exchanged a word since you left, Joe," Sheila reported. "How did Ms Randleson take the news?"

Joe gulped down a mouthful of beer. "Odd. She's shipped into this place with the dead woman, and yet they hardly know each other, according to her."

"Then what brought them together?" Brenda asked. "Horizontal exercise?"

Sheila tutted. "Does your mind ever stray above waist level, Brenda?"

"Yes, but not very often." Brenda focused on Joe. "Well?"

"I thought the same thing, but that's not the way it is, according to the Randleson woman. For certain, she didn't look too upset to learn that her chalet mate had been topped."

"I've seen that look on your face before, Joe Murray. Suspicion." Sheila glanced anxiously at her watch. "I wish the police would hurry up and get here. I'd like to get back to my digs."

Joe hesitated a moment, but eventually said, "I don't know whether they'll let you leave, Sheila. They might insist that you stay here for the night."

She shook her head. "No way. I have no intention of staying in this place overnight. For all I care, they can arrest me and throw me in a cell, I am not stopping here."

"Don't be stupid," Brenda chided. "You don't have a problem staying here tonight, Sheila, and I'm sure the police will let you go back to your bed-and-breakfast first thing in the morning."

"I don't have any night clothes with me. I don't have a change of clothing for tomorrow. They're all back at my B&B."

Sheila looked to Joe who shrugged. "I'll see what I can do for you. According to Edström, it was Kirsty Hinch who put him onto us. She's been promoted to inspector, and the chances are, she'll be the SIO. If that's so, I'll have a word, but no guarantees."

"That is so unfair. You know it's nothing to do with me, Joe, just the same as I know it's nothing to do with either of you. Good heavens, we've been together since five o'clock this afternoon, and according to you, the woman's only been dead an hour."

Joe felt his irritation rising again. He got to his feet. "I'll go get us a drink. Just remind us, Sheila, how long were you married to a police inspector?" He tromped moodily off to the bar.

Brenda remained unapologetic. "He does have a point, dear. Most of the time it's you telling us that we should obey the instructions of the police. You don't need to worry about nightwear. I have a spare nightie you can borrow, and if they do hold you here, I'm sure they'll let you go early tomorrow. Let's just see what they have to say when they get here." She sighed and glanced towards the bar. "I think Joe's going to be the bigger problem. We came here to look into thefts, and now he has a murder on his hands, and you know what he's like. He'll be on a pleasure overload close to orgasm."

"And any chance we have of a few peaceful days in Skegness will be gone."

Chapter Nine

Kirsty Hinch had mixed feelings about the text message coming in from her sergeant at quarter to nine.

She had already sat through an hour or more of King Lear, and found it lacking entertainment value (she did not like Shakespeare as a matter of choice) and disagreeable in places. Lear was prattling about a thankless child being sharper than a serpent's tooth, when her phone vibrated to silently announce the incoming message. On the other hand, she didn't like to walk out on her partner barely halfway through the evening's entertainment.

Possible murder. Sun Kissed, the message read.

She texted her sergeant back immediately. *I'm at the Rep. Pick me up outside*, and then whispered to her partner that she had to leave. "Sorry. Have to go. Business. Serious crime."

Ignoring his annoyance, bending low, shuffling past the other spectators on the row, apologising for disturbing them, she hurried from the theatre and as she stepped out into the warm night, her sergeant's car pulled up in front of the theatre. She climbed into the passenger seat.

"Foot down, fairy lights on, and, tell me what you know."

Detective Sergeant Nigel Brightwood obeyed.

Twenty-six years of age, he reminded Kirsty of herself in the days when she was a DC, later a sergeant. Barely out of university, a few years working in Lincoln behind him, first in uniform and then earning his spurs in CID before moving back to his hometown of Skegness, and eventual promotion to Detective Sergeant when Dudley Nichols moved on. Smartly turned out, intelligent, perhaps too aggressive on occasion, he was a man who helped her get results, and a man destined for the rank of inspector in years to come.

At least, that was her opinion, but as she was so often at pains to point out, they had never yet dealt with anything truly serious. If the reports from Sun Kissed were correct, this would be a litmus test for both of them.

As he drove along, heading south out of the town towards Gibraltar Point, he brought her up to date.

"Håkan Edström rang in just before I contacted you. He rang the station direct, not 999. He has a dead woman in the toilets, throat cut. That's all he knows. Apparently he has some kind of smartarse private detective staying there, and he advised them."

Kirsty's hopes rose. "Joe Murray. I recommended him to Edström earlier this week. And for reference, Nigel, Joe isn't a smartarse... Well, he is, but when he speaks, you listen."

"He's that good, is he, guv?"

"You probably don't remember the Hamlet murders from a few years ago."

"I was in Lincoln at the time, but I remember reading about them."

"Yeah, well, it was Joe Murray who cracked it. If it hadn't been for him, we'd have settled for an old biddy shuffling them all off and then topping herself, but Murray saw through a fake suicide note, and pinned the killer down. Dud Nichols took the credit, naturally. He was SIO. But trust me, it was all down to Joe Murray and his two concubines."

Brightwood laughed. "Two? Isn't one woman enough for him?"

"According to legend, they're just good friends."

"Yeah, and I've been calling on the Chief Constable's wife for a while, when her old man's at work."

They were heading out of town, into the near darkness of unlit streets when Kirsty changed the subject. "Have you sent forensic out?"

"Ordered them right away, ma'am, and I let the pathologist know. Five'll get you ten, they're all there before us."

"You know the score at Sun Kissed, do you?"

Brightwood's face darkened. "Nudists, aren't they?" His

cynicism showed through his next words. "Crap excuse for bed-hopping if you want my opinion."

"That's what I like to hear. An unbiased police officer fully acquainted with the modern world." She gave vent to her irritation. "It is not an excuse for bed-hopping, as you put it. It's a way of life for these people, and there are rules, Nigel, especially for visitors, and the most important rule is, don't stare. I don't give a toss how big a top set some young woman has, no ogling. Understand?"

The severity of her warning called him to order. "Yes, ma'am." Silence prevailed for a few moments before he asked, "What's this Murray sort doing there?"

"Edström's had more than his fair share of thieving. He came to see me on Monday and I told him I can't prioritise it. Hell, we don't have enough bodies to deal with the crap going off in the town as it is. Anyway, I recommended he call in Joe Murray, and I'm assuming he's done so. In fact, I'm assuming that this alleged private investigator is Joe Murray. I don't know it for a fact."

"And if it is, you'll be happy for him to poke his nose in, will you?"

"It'll be almost impossible to stop him."

Brightwood was right on one point. When they turned into the Sun Kissed Holiday Park, the white vans of the CSI team were already there, and parked alongside them was pathologist, Frank Greenall's car – well known to them – and a black mortuary van, marked 'Private Ambulance'.

"Looks like it's for real," Kirsty said as she climbed out of the car, and made for the boot. She raised the lid and looked down in dismay. "Forensic jumpsuits, Nigel?"

"Oh. Sorry, boss. I was at home when I got the call, and I came straight to the Rep to pick you up."

She wagged an admonishing finger at him. "You should never have less than two sets in your car. Now, while I talk to Edström and his wife, get in there and ask forensics for two sets."

"Yes, ma'am."

Kirsty strode into the building and rang the bell on

reception. A few moments later, Edström appeared and to her relief, he was fully dressed.

"Inspector Hinch." Edström offered his hand and Kirsty shook it. "It's good to see you again, but I wish it were under happier circumstances."

"Me, too, Håkan. I'm told you mentioned a private detective over the phone. Did you take my advice?"

"I did, and I'm glad I did. We have a doctor staying here, but when we called her in, she was ill at ease. Mr Murray on the other hand… ah, there is a man in complete control of himself and the situation. He assured us she was dead, Dr Coll confirmed it, and that's when I rang you."

"I'm waiting for forensic coveralls, after which I'll take a look at the scene, and then I'll need to speak to this doctor, and Joe. You say the doctor is female?"

Edström nodded. "Dr Delia Coll. She's from the same area as Joe Murray and his two friends. Somewhere in Yorkshire."

"All right, Håkan. Here's the situation. Thursday night and I know Saturday is changeover day and in view of what's happened, a number of your guests may be inclined to leave beforehand, but no one, absolutely no one can leave this site until we've spoken to them. I'll make that clear to your guests. The dead woman. Staff? Guest?"

"The latter, although, as you know, we refer to them as members."

Kirsty ignored the point. "You won't be allowed to let anyone in her chalet until our people are finished there, and that could be Monday morning. The woman's name?"

"Renata Chappell. She's staying with another, recently enrolled permanent member, Diane Randleson."

"Then I'm afraid Ms Randleson will not be allowed to return to her chalet. Do you have room to accommodate her for the night?"

"I suppose we shall have to cope. It will be difficult. The height of the season and we're fully booked from Saturday."

Kirsty gave him a wan smile. "We'll try to ensure we're through by then, but to be honest, that's not my problem. However, we will be as quick as we can. One last thing, and

I'll be relying on you to get the message across to your guests, er, members. We will need to interview everyone, and while they're with us, they will need to wear some kind of clothing. I don't care if it's only a bathing costume."

Edström frowned. "Mr Murray insisted on the same thing, and it goes against our underlying principles, Inspector."

"And as of now this entire site is now a crime scene, sir, and I am in charge, and nudity while giving a statement is against my underlying principles."

A knock on the door, followed by Brightwood's entry, ended the discussion. The sergeant passed a set of forensic coveralls and overshoes to Kirsty, and they both proceeded to suit up. When they were ready, Kirsty asked Edström to show them the way, and he led them from the office along the narrow corridor, past the bar entrance, and the ladies restroom, where Kirsty insisted he wait outside, while she and Brightwood went into the toilets.

It was a cramped and crowded environment. Forensic officers stood by, waiting for the medical examiner, Greenall, to finish taking his readings and samples, a photographer was busy in the background, aiming his lens at the tiled floor and pools of drying blood.

Greenall looked up. "Good evening, Ms Hinch. Not so good for this young lady, I'm afraid."

"Cause of death?"

Greenall gestured at the livid cut across Renata Chappell's trachea. "Airway sliced open, compounded by exsanguination I shouldn't wonder. I'll give you the precise cause of death once I've worked on her, but it may be Monday before I get round to the post-mortem." A grimace from Brightwood caught his attention. "Unlike you, Sergeant, I don't get paid overtime for working weekends." Greenall focussed on Kirsty, and gave her an apologetic smile. "No offence, Inspector, but I feel this case will be more about the who and the why rather than the how."

"Yes, well, we're about to start quizzing the members. Can you give me an idea regarding the time of death?"

"Not long." Greenall checked his watch. "It's a quarter to

ten. I would say no earlier than half past eight, more likely closer to nine o'clock."

"Thanks, Doc."

Kirsty stepped around the doctor, into the far corner, and looked down upon Renata. A fulsome figure, a little heavy in the breast and thigh, first signs of flab developing around the midriff, her eyes were wide open. Disbelief. It was a sign Kirsty had seen on previous occasions, most of them the result of accidents. Total shock that her life was about to end at least thirty years too early.

"Nigel, get onto Edström. He must have records of her. I want to see them. I want every detail about her."

"Right, guv."

"When you've done that, get onto the station, asked them to send a few uniforms out here to take statements. I'll be in the bar speaking to the crowd."

"Roger that."

Brightwood disappeared and Greenall looked up from his crouched position. "You're angry, young Kirsty."

"You bet. How old would you say she is, Doc? I reckon she's about forty. Too young to be left in this state in a public lavatory. If you need me, I'll be with Edström and his guests."

Still irritated, she left the restroom, and made her way back towards the office, but diverted into the bar. She was about to introduce herself when Brightwood appeared at her side, followed by Edström.

The sergeant kept his voice low. "Just spoken to Mr Edström, ma'am, and he gave the files to your pal, Murray earlier today."

"Right. Thanks, Nigel." She faced the crowd in the bar. "Ladies and gentlemen, may I have your attention please?" Silence fell and all eyes turned upon her. "I am Detective Inspector Hinch, Skegness CID. You've all been made aware that there has been a suspicious death on site, and it's my job to find out exactly what happened. Officers will arrive soon to take statements from you. In the meantime, no one can leave this room, except to visit the toilet, and for that you will be accompanied by a police officer or a member of Mr Edström's staff. In addition, I must insist that you do not contact anyone by telephone. Since the incident is not yet public knowledge, you don't have to inform relatives that you're safe. For now, I need to speak to three people: Diane Randleson, Dr Delia Coll, and Joe Murray. Mr Murray, we'll deal with you first. If you'd like to accompany me to Mr Edström's office."

From the rear of the room, Joe got to his feet, had a brief word with Sheila and Brenda, and then made his way out, through the fire door, and followed Kirsty to the main office.

Once seated, she beamed a smile of welcome upon him. "God, it's good to see you again, Joe."

"You too, Kirsty. An inspector now. What happened to not-so-cuddly Dudley Nichols?"

"He moved on to a serious crime squad covering the entire county. With luck and a following wind, we won't see anything of him. I don't wanna rush you, Joe, but I need to get down to business, and Edström tells us that he gave all the files relating to his guests to you. I'm gonna need them."

"They're in our chalet. I'd go get them for you, but you've already said we're not allowed to leave the bar."

"That's no problem. Come on. Let's take a walk over there."

To avoid going through the bar, they left via the public entrance, which opened out onto the swimming pool on the semicircle of chalets.

"I'm not too surprised to see you here," Kirsty said, "because I recommended you to Edström when he came to see me earlier in the week. Did he tell you that this is a naturist site?"

Joe laughed. "No. But to be fair, he tried to. I just didn't give him the chance."

"So how are you and your two ladies getting on with all the flesh on display?"

He laughed again. "Sheila and I are looking in every other direction, and Brenda's taking notes."

Now Kirsty laughed. "You're a dark horse, Joe Murray."

"Maybe I am. Oh, while I think on. Sheila. She's struggling to deal with the naturist angle, and she shipped out to stay in a B&B. She had serious issues with staying here tonight. Is there any chance you can get a statement from her early, and let her go back to her digs?"

"Can she tell us anything?"

"Probably not. And whatever she can tell you, Brenda and I can give you the bottom line."

"Then I don't see a problem."

Joe arrived at chalet #17, and was immediately alarmed to find the door slightly ajar. Without waiting for Kirsty, he rushed in, found the place in darkness, and then ferreted for the light switch.

Kirsty checked the door. "Not forced, so it was someone with a key."

With the lights on, his worst fear was immediately apparent. The place was a mess. The files, which Sheila had left on the table, were missing. A check on the bedroom revealed that the cases belonging to him and Brenda, had been upturned and rifled and his laptop was gone.

"Damn and blast."

"The files, Joe?"

"Taken. Along with everything else." He returned to the main room, and checked the shelf above the fake fire, from where he retrieved his hidden mini camera. "But at least I have this."

Chapter Ten

During the time Joe and Kirsty were absent, a small team of uniformed officers arrived, and were setting about the process of taking statements from the members.

Joe was in a mean mood when they returned to the bar, but Kirsty told him to hold his complaints, and called for the Edströms, Sheila, Brenda, and Brightwood, then led them to the reception area.

"Mr Edström's office is too small for us all to squeeze in comfortably," she explained. "Now that we're all here, I'll leave it to Joe to tell you what's happened."

He concentrated more on his two friends than he did the Edströms or the sergeant. "While we were in the bar, dining room, someone with a key went into our chalet. They've taken everything. My laptop, your files, Håkan, God knows what other bits and pieces you might have had lying around, Brenda, and they turned our luggage inside out. The place is a right bloody mess." He faced Edström. "I'm sorry, Håkan. We had the place covered with a camera, and the chances are we will have them, but what's happened to your files, I don't know."

Edström tutted, but his wife was more vehement. "We could be in big trouble here. Loss of personal information, and it could be construed as an infringement of the data protection act. When we handed you the files, we expected you to take more care of them."

"And how the hell was I supposed to know someone would raid our chalet?" It was an excuse, and Joe knew it. He should have stored the files safely away or even brought them back to reception and handed them to Edström.

"Save the inquest for later," Kirsty said, in an effort to

maintain control of the situation. "Right now, we have a number of problems, the primary one being that any information we have on Renata Chappell is gone. We know nothing about her."

Sheila held up a finger. "That's not quite true, Inspector. I'd already done some work on the files, and I have that information stored on my iPad."

"Which was in the chalet," Joe said.

Sheila promptly disabused them of the notion. "No it wasn't. I put it back in my car before we came out for dinner. Unlike you, Joe, when I'm away, I always keep these things safe. Good heavens, when you were in Cornwall and I was on honeymoon, wasn't Les Tanner robbed, and didn't you warn him about leaving expensive personal equipment lying around his caravan?"

Joe held up his hands at chest height, a gesture of surrender. "All right, all right. So we shouldn't have left these things kicking around the chalet, but I've just said that whoever the thief is, he went through our luggage, so no matter where we kept them, he would have found and taken them."

"It would have been better if you had returned the files to us," Edström said.

Once again, Kirsty called them to order. "Ladies, gentlemen, can we knock it off, please. I said, we can deal with the inquest later. For now, we can look at the footage from your camera, Joe—"

He cut her off. "You can, but its internal memory is tiny, and if it died before he broke in, chances are there'll be nothing on it but a neat and tidy chalet."

"Nevertheless, we'll look at it." She eyed Sheila. "I need to know about Renata Chappell, Mrs Riley. What can you tell us?"

"I'll need to go to my car to get the iPad."

Kirsty ordered her sergeant, "Nigel, go with her. It's not that I don't trust you, Sheila, but bearing in mind everything that's happened, I have to ensure your safety."

Sheila and Brightwood left the area, and Kirsty

concentrated on Edström. "The theft of this information and equipment from Joe's chalet. Is it similar to the other thefts your guests have reported?"

"It sounds similar, but I don't remember anyone complaining that the thieves had gone through their luggage."

Kirsty's attention swung back to Joe. "I don't suppose you've made any progress on the thefts?"

"We've only been here seven hours. We got as far as deciding to check out the staff and we'd spoken to a few guests, those who were robbery victims—"

"Members," Margot interrupted to correct him.

"Whatever you want to call on them, we spoke to them, and I set up the camera, which was linked to my laptop."

"A laptop you were supposed to bring with you when we stepped out for dinner, and which you forgot," Brenda pointed out.

"I thought it would be safe in the bedroom." Reading the doubt on Brenda's face, Joe shrugged. "Okay. It looks like I'm the whipping boy tonight. What are you gonna do for an encore? Charge me with murdering this woman in the khasi?"

"How many people knew why you were here?" Kirsty asked.

"Everyone. We were quite open about it."

Joe was still thinking about expanding on his answer when Brenda spoke up. "More specifically, there was Margot, Håkan, and Carol Liddle."

Joe blanched, Brenda put her hand to her mouth, and the Edströms both frowned.

"She means Margot and Håkan," Joe said in the hope of forestalling the inevitable.

He failed. "Carol who?" Margot asked.

Her husband echoed the sentiment. "I know all of my members, both permanent and casual, and there is no Carol Liddle staying here."

Kirsty looked to Joe, then to Brenda, and back to Joe. "Well?"

Joe and Brenda were locked in a silent stare, each asking the other what the correct course of action should be. Eventually, Joe spoke up.

"Doctor Delia Coll is not a doctor. Her name is Carol Liddle. She's an investigative reporter who works for the West Yorkshire Chronicle. We've come across her before. We know what she's doing here but she point blank refused to go into detail. I recognised her the moment I saw her this afternoon, and Brenda and I tackled her. We had to. She knows us of old, and if we let everyone know who she is, she'd have pasted us in the newspapers."

Brenda took up the narrative. "All she told us was that she's onto a big story. That's it. That's as much as we know."

"Not a doctor." Margot huffed out her breath. "No wonder she was so reluctant to check out the dead woman."

"One thing I can tell you," Joe said. "Whoever killed this woman, it wasn't likely to be Carol Liddle. You'll know more when you've got a proper time of death, Kirsty, but Liddle was in the dining room not long after us, and she didn't move until Margot asked her to check the dead woman."

Margot was quick to accuse. "And you were quick to go with her, Mr Murray."

"I had to. I said we needed to keep quiet about her to prevent us and you becoming the lead in next Sunday's tabloids. That, Mrs Edström, was in your best interests. We know this woman, and if she'd gone to the toilet alone, with you, you'd have realised in seconds that she wasn't a doctor and she'd have made certain the rest of the place was hammered as a haven of… of… iniquity. She'd have made you look like the madam of an expensive brothel. Trust me. I know this woman. We've had grief with her before. She's a spiteful, vindictive bag, especially when she doesn't get her way."

"All right, all right," Kirsty intervened. "We can stand here arguing the toss all night, it won't get us any further forward." She concentrated on Joe. "I don't know that the two incidents – the murder and the thefts – are linked, but I want to take a look at whatever footage your camera has—"

"It'll be nothing. I told you the camera doesn't have a big —"

"You might also find, Joe, that it operates on a movement sensor. It only kicks in when it detects movement."

"Oh. I didn't know that."

Kirsty chuckled. "You paid for this camera and didn't bother to learn how it works?"

Brenda was less impressed. "He's always doing it. He bought a barista machine for the café a year or two back, and he still doesn't have a clue what to do with it."

"I employ you and the others to handle it."

Kirsty brought them to order again. "The minute Sergeant Brightwood gets back with Mrs Riley's iPad, we'll see what we can learn about the victim. Joe, you were here at ground zero. According to the pathologist, she was murdered sometime around half-eight, nine-ish. Is there anyone at all you can exonerate?"

Joe contemplated the question for a moment. "I just mentioned Liddle, and there's an old boy on the table next to us, Ignatius someone or other."

"Ignatius Isherwood," Edström said. "Everyone knows him as Aye-Aye."

"That's him," Joe said. "He all but propositioned Sheila and Brenda, but the waiter, Ellis, told us to ignore him. He never moved. Carol Liddle was sat with the woman, Randleson."

"Diane Randleson," Margot said.

"Neither of them moved until Margot asked Carol to check the dead woman."

"And Ms Randleson didn't move at all after that," Brenda said. "Not until Joe and Håkan came to take her into the office and tell her what had happened."

"Do you know anything about her, Mr Edström?"

"She's a permanent member. Strange woman. She has no objection to nudity, but refuses to step outside other than when she's wearing a bathing costume. Beyond that, Inspector, as always, we know very little."

Joe concentrated on Kirsty. "You're absolutely certain of

the time of death, are you?"

"Nothing like. Our Medical Examiner's just given us a spec opinion. We won't know for sure until he does the post-mortem. Even then, Joe, you know as well as I do, that pinning down the time of death is little better than educated speculation."

"All I can tell you is that the body was warm when I got to it, but hey, what do I know? I'm being blamed for everything else right now, so maybe I topped her and kept her in an oven."

Kirsty ignored his final complaint. "What time was that?"

"It would have been about… oh, getting on for nine. Or thereabouts." He looked to Brenda for confirmation, and she nodded.

Kirsty turned her attention to Edström. "Do you have somewhere I can use as a base?"

He disappeared into the rear office, and reappeared a moment later with a set of keys, which he handed to her. "Chalet number one. It's free, at least for tonight and tomorrow."

Kirsty took the keys and turned to Joe. "Come on, let's take a look at this camera of yours."

Brenda grinned and nudged him. "Hey up, Joe. A lady policeman giving you the come on."

He dismissed her with a scowl and followed Kirsty from reception, first to Brightwood's car, where she collected a laptop, and then back into the semicircle of chalets.

Joe glanced at his watch, realised that it was after ten o'clock. The sun had set twenty minutes previously, but above the sky was still a blaze of pearly twilight, with a glorious orange/red showing over the roof of the reception building. And it was not much cooler than it had been during the day.

Kirsty let them into chalet #1, Joe flicked on the lights, and they settled at the table. While waiting for the laptop to go through its boot routine, he looked around. It was furnished in exactly the same manner as number seventeen, right down to the quirky, absurd ornaments above the fireplace.

Before many minutes had passed, Kirsty had the machine running, and downloaded the footage the camera had stored in its small memory.

As Kirsty had hinted, it operated on passive sensors, the camera activating only when someone passed within range. As a result, there was less than five minutes of dark footage. The camera had a night vision setting which had kicked in automatically, and the intruder was plain enough to see. He was much taller than Joe, but he was clad – Joe was certain it was a man – from head to foot in black, including a black balaclava which hid his face. He was also wearing black gloves.

"Not much point sending the dab men in," Kirsty said, "but I'll get the CSI guys to go over your place. You never know. With a bit of luck, he might have left us something to work on. I'm sorry, Joe, but there's nothing to indicate that this incident was linked to the woman's murder."

"You think not? What about the files that were stolen?"

"I can see what you're saying, but come on, Joe, this is the twenty-first century. Identity theft is big business, even for the little guys. Files like that are a gold mine to any thief. If – and I stress the word – if this theft is linked to Renata Chappell's murder, it means that we're not looking for one person, but two."

"On the basis that she was killed in the ladies toilet?"

"Exactly. I mean, it's not entirely impossible to imagine some guy sneaking into the ladies, but if anyone saw him, he'd be deep in the do-do." She handed Joe his camera. "Best thing we can do, my friend, is leave this on the backburner for now, and see how the inquiry develops. In the meantime, I'd better get Brightwood here with Mrs Riley's iPad. Especially if we're to get her back to her digs tonight." She chuckled. "What is it about this place that she can't handle? The nudity?"

"Got it in one. Mind, she's not on her own. I have trouble with it, too, and although she says different, I think Brenda does."

Kirsty laughed. "Odd. I always figured Brenda as quite lively in, er... How can I put this politely?"

Joe recalled Brenda's description. "Horizontal exercise?"

"That's about right."

"Yeah, well, that's usually in the dark, not queueing up at the bar for a pint."

"Right, well... Oh. While I think on. This reporter woman, Carol Liddle, did you say her name is? Is she really as bad as you make out?"

"Probably worse. We've had a few set to's, and the worst was in Blackpool just before New Year. She abides by the tabloid doctrine of not letting trivia like the truth to get in the way of the story. Her boss was compelled to print an apology to me after Blackpool because she got it all wrong." His face fell. "Yeah, but it didn't stop them printing the tale."

"Don't worry about her, Joe. She's in for a nasty surprise in a few minutes when I speak to her. For the time being, I'd appreciate any help you can give me, and please, keep your contact with the outside world to a minimum. Okay?"

"You've got it."

Chapter Eleven

With Sheila's agreement, Kirsty downloaded copies of the information from the iPad to her laptop, after which, Brightwood took a statement from Sheila before she was allowed to leave the site.

Joe immediately spoke up. "Kirsty, would you mind if Brenda and I accompanied Sheila? I'm thinking of her safety, naturally, and we'll be back within the hour, as long as that's all right with you."

It was obvious from the scowl on Brightwood's face that he disapproved, but Kirsty, knowing Joe and his two friends as she did, had no hesitation. "As long as you and Mrs Jump are back here tonight, I don't mind. You're not suspects, but you three are at the heart of this investigation, and you're also victims, if only of theft. I want you here."

Joe saluted. "My word of honour as a boy scout."

The three friends made their way back to the chalet, and out to the rear, where Brenda climbed into Sheila's Fiat, and Joe prepared to follow them. But before they left, he gave instructions.

"On the way back to your digs, look out for a pub. I'd like a quiet drink between us where we can talk openly."

"No problem," Sheila said. "Well there is. You were never in the scouts."

"She doesn't know that, and it was the only way I could think of guaranteeing that we'll be back. Now stop nit-picking and let's get for a beer. Oh, and we'll need your iPad when we get to…wherever we end up."

Ready to climb into Sheila's passenger seat, Brenda smiled, "I love it when Joe's so precise, don't you?"

"If you don't get a move on the bars will be shut," Joe told her, and got into his car.

As it turned out, they were almost back in Skegness before they found a hotel where the bar was open to the public. Joe arranged drinks for them, a gin and tonic for Sheila, Campari and soda for Brenda, and a half of lager for himself, they settled into a corner booth, where they could talk with comparative freedom.

Sheila took out her iPad, but first, Joe brought them up to speed with the break-in at their chalet.

"It was definitely a man?" Sheila asked.

"Either that or a very tall and flat-chested woman doing a good impression. I mean, nothing's guaranteed, but the balance of probability says the thief was a man. What Kirsty won't have is that the break-in was linked to the death of Renata Chappell."

"No evidence," Brenda said. "And she's right, Joe. Just forgetting the break-in for a moment, who was favourite for murdering this Chappell woman?"

"The betting's wide open," Joe said. "There are people we know it couldn't have been. Carol Liddle, the one, the woman she was sat with, Diane wossname... Randleson. Then there's the old duffer on the table next to us, Aye-Aye, or whatever you want to call him."

"Ignatius Isherwood," Sheila said. "There was a couple with him, wasn't there?"

"Arabella Simpson and Bill Welsby," Joe said, and he noticed Sheila's eyebrows rise. "Brenda and I interviewed them earlier in the afternoon."

"Oh. Okay. And we can eliminate them with the others can we?"

"No, we can't," Brenda said. "They were with Aye-Aye for dinner but they left soon after they finished eating, and they were nowhere to be seen when Margot came screaming in. The same goes for the other couple, Joe, Kesteven and Ormond, and that bloke you thought might be conning his insurance company."

"Trevor Pollitt," Joe said.

Sheila's frustration began to grown. "Aside from these

people is there anyone else we can eliminate on the grounds that they were under observation when Margot came in screaming her head off that there was a dead body in the toilet?"

Brenda laughed. "As opposed to a live body in the toilet?"

Joe clucked again. "And you talk about me side-tracking the debate. And you're wrong, Sheila. Yes, we can eliminate Randleson, Liddle and the old boy. We know Simpson and Welsby, Pollitt, Kesteven and Ormond all went AWOL shortly after dinner, along with a few others. At best we've eliminated, what, half a dozen people, including ourselves, but there must be at least another hundred on site. On the other hand, I'm focussing on the five I've already mentioned. They're our most likely suspects, and out of them, I'd say Pollitt is favourite."

The two women exchanged a surprised gaze, and Brenda turned and faced Joe again. "Why do you say that?"

Joe needed to consider his response. He drained his glass, and made his way to the bar where he bought a fresh round of drinks. By the time he returned to the table he was ready.

"According to Edström these thefts have been going on for about three months. That's all that's happened. We arrived today, he announces us to the world, and the next thing we know, one of the members is murdered. And yet, Kirsty Hinch won't accept that the two issues are linked."

"You already said, Joe," Brenda responded. "There's no evidence."

"Oh, so you don't think it's a bit too coincidental?"

Sheila would not hear it. "Not where we're concerned. Practically everywhere we go with the 3rd Age Club, we end up investigating a murder."

Joe strummed his lips. "Hmm. I never thought of that." He shook his head. "Nope. I won't have it. Here's the way I see it. Renata is – was the resident tea leaf, and rather than hawking the stuff off, she had a look at these missing laptops, and discovered information which would be more profitable than flogging the machine to a second hand shop. So she turned the screws on Pollitt, demanded a payoff." Joe looked to Brenda for support. "You were there when he said he doesn't declare every last penny to the taxman."

"Yes, but that's not to say he was making a fortune. We could be talking pennies, Joe."

"For the sake of argument, let's assume we're not. I mean, it doesn't have to be something to do with his livelihood. It could be anything. Now, to take the argument further. Under any other circumstances Pollitt might tell her to get stuffed, but he knows there are three private investigators on site: us, and he's worried that we might get to the bottom of the problem, get a look at his laptop, and we learn what it is he's trying to hide."

There was a fairly long silence before Sheila finally spoke up. "I can see what you're getting at, Joe, but you're stretching a point. We don't know that Renata was a thief, we don't know that Pollitt has any great secret, and remember, Renata wasn't here alone. Diane Randleson was with her. Or are you saying that Diane's involved too?"

"It's all there to be proven, and you can help, Sheila. I don't expect you to come back to Sun Kissed, but can you start digging into as many of the others as you can, just to see if anything turns up?"

"And not only him," Brenda said. "But Welsby, Simpson, Kesteven, and Ormond."

Sheila yawned. "Right, yes, I get the message, but it will have to be tomorrow. I'm tired and I need a good night's sleep."

Brenda drained her second glass, Joe followed suit. "All right," Joe said. "Ring us in the morning when you're up and about, Sheila, and we'll meet somewhere for breakfast." Now he yawned. "Right now, I need to get back down there, and like you, grab a decent night's kip."

Brenda sulked. "Looks like I'm in for a boring night, doesn't it?"

Joe ignored the comment and soon after, with Sheila's agreement to meet at breakfast anywhere but Sun Kissed, they parted company on the hotel car park, Sheila driving off to her digs, Joe and Brenda climbing into his car for the journey back to the holiday park, and as they drove along, Brenda kept up her complaints about the lack of attention to her 'needs' as she tagged them.

"You're very tempting, Brenda. You always are, but honestly, I'm whacked. And you should be, too. We've both been on the go since half six, seven o'clock this morning."

"Tsk. You know me. I'm young and lively… for my age, and all this flesh, Joe. It's making me feel frisky."

"And you're the one who tells us that naturism is nothing to do with sex."

"I can dream, can't I?"

"Well, carry on dreaming. Hey, maybe I can fix you up with old Aye-Aye."

She snorted. "He'd never last the night with me, and I think Sun Kissed has enough with one corpse, don't you?" She yawned. "Maybe you're right, though. A good night's kip and by tomorrow my batteries will be fully charged, and you'll have to make sure you've sharpened the lead in your pencil."

Their plans changed the moment they arrived at the park and gazed upon a scene of mayhem.

Two uniformed officers were struggling to get a woman into the back of a patrol car, and they realised that the woman was Carol Liddle in full flow and screaming abuse at full volume.

"Credit where it's due," Brenda said as they climbed out of the car. "That woman certainly knows how to curse. She could put the entire Parachute Regiment to shame."

Unable to pass the array of police vehicles, Joe parked off to one side, and they climbed out, watching with interest while Carol Liddle placed her foot against the door of the police car in an effort to stop the male and female officers from pressing her into the back seat. She resisted, she delivered a voluble and audible flow of Anglo-Saxon, but it served no purpose other than to delay the inevitable, before they squeezed her into the car, and closed the doors.

Kirsty Hinch was stood by watching events.

"What's she done to upset you?" Joe asked.

"Not me. Nick-Nick."

Joe frowned. "Who?"

"Nichols. You remember him. What was it you called him? Not so cuddly Dudley. My boss when we were looking into the murders at the Rep. And I'm glad you're here because he needs to talk to you."

"About Liddle?"

"About what Liddle was investigating. Or should I say who Liddle was investigating."

Joe laughed, a short, sharp bark. "He didn't ask her? Or didn't he hear the answer through all the swearing and cursing?"

"Oh, he asked, but she wouldn't tell him. She gave him a mouthful of abuse instead, and eventually, Dudley lost it. And if you don't tell him what you know, Joe, he'll arrest you as well. And you, Brenda. That's the kind of mood he's in."

"Well, he's wasting his time," Brenda said. "Liddle didn't tell us anything."

"You'd better hope he believes that. Come on. I'll take you through."

She led them into reception and behind the counter to the Edströms' office where DCI Dudley Nichols was pacing the floor, one ear to his phone. He was listening rather than speaking confining himself to repeats of 'yes, sir', 'no, sir', over and over again, and Joe recalled that the last time they met, he was also on the phone, but as he remembered it was a personal call.

His close-cropped hair was a little longer now and according to Joe's estimate, he would be in his early forties. The irritation knitted through his brow and burning through his eyes said he would prefer not to defer to the party on the other end of the line, but he had no choice. He stood over six feet, his body slender but for the faintest hint of a spread at the waist, and while he listened and responded, his free hand clenched and unclenched.

Joe smiled to himself. This was exactly the kind of police officer he loved to meet head on.

Nichols ended the call, glared at his smartphone, and snapped, "Daft old git." He fixed Kirsty in his gaze, got to his feet, and raised his eyebrows.

"Joe Murray and Brenda Jump, guv."

The fire in Nichols's eyes became more predatory. "You are gonna tell me everything you know."

Without waiting for an invitation, Joe pulled out two chairs, sat Brenda down, and took the one next to her. "All right, Nichols, where do we start? I was born a long time ago, and I don't really have any memories before I was about five years old, and by then, the pit in Sanford was ready for closing down, but I'll tell you everything I know from there."

Frustration burst through Nichols's words. "What are you talking about, man?"

"Well, you said you wanted to know everything we know. But I'm older than you, so I probably know a lot more, and we'll be here for hours while I tell you all about it. And then we'll have to wait for Brenda's story."

"I'm talking about Carol Liddle, you idiot."

Brenda spoke at this time. "When it comes to idiocy, Chief Inspector, I reckon you stole a march on us. What we know about Carol Liddle can be summed up in just a few words. We hate her and she hates us. That's it. Can we get off to bed now?"

The deliberate confabulation was already getting to Nichols, and alongside Joe and Brenda, Kirsty struggled to rein in her giggly humour.

"I want to know what she told you about the mark she was investigating."

"Nothing," Joe declared. "We recognised her, she recognised us. She told us she had a big story coming down, and nothing more than that."

Nichols's threatening finger pointing at them. "If you're covering for her—"

Joe cut the chief inspector off. "No way would we ever cover for her. Cover her up, yes, but only with six inches of concrete. I've just told you what she told us, but you know what puzzles me. Why didn't you ask her?"

"I did. She wouldn't tell me. That's why she's on her way to the nick."

Kirsty spoke up. "Wouldn't it be better, sir, if you told us exactly what is going on? I mean, you don't have to name names or anything like that, but I can't understand why you would haul a reporter off just because she's working undercover."

Nichols dropped into the seat behind the desk, and a lengthy silence followed. Eventually, he focused on Joe and Brenda. "She didn't tell you who she was watching?"

Joe left it to Brenda. "She told us it was someone high in government circles. She used the words 'Right Honourable' so maybe it's an MP or something. That was all we got out of her. We have an agreement. Joe and I are working here as private eyes, looking into a spate of thefts on this site. Everyone's aware of that, but we know her of old, and she knows us, so we had to strike a deal. We keep our mouths shut about her, she keeps her mouth shut about our progress."

"I did press her for the mark's identity," Joe said, taking up the narrative, "but she wouldn't tell us anything beyond what Brenda's just said. According to her, the story could hit the nationals big style."

Now Kirsty intervened. "And the next thing I know, you turned up, Dudley. And that means someone on this site rang to complain about her, and that can only have happened after Mrs Jump revealed Liddle's real identity, and after I'd given instructions that no one was to speak to anyone other than my officers."

Nichols sighed and aimed a shaking finger at his phone. "That was the Chief Constable's office giving me earache, and you're right, Kirsty. I can't tell you who the person is, because I'm not allowed to, but this person is high up in government circles. The likes of you and me would need oxygen to breathe at that level. The CC got a phone call from someone in London. Cabinet Office, maybe even MI5. I'm damned if I know. I was ordered to clamp down on this story now. Not tomorrow, not a week on Tuesday, now. Not only that, I was instructed to find out who the source was, and this stupid tart wouldn't tell me. Journalistic code of practice. They never reveal their sources. Well, that's fine, because I don't really care. For all I care she can rot in jail for the next twenty years."

"But Kirsty told you that we were the ones who exposed her real identity?" Joe asked.

Nichols nodded. "Before you go blaming her, Murray, she was following my orders."

Joe smiled. "I would never blame her, Nichols. Not while you and I are in the same room. So, what is it that's so important about this bod Liddle was investigating?"

"He... or she has more brains than you. She... or he listens when other people speak. And I said once, I can't tell you who it is or what is so important about him... or her."

Brenda gave vent to her feelings. "Another Westminster wallah guilty of moral terpsichory."

"Turpitude," Joe corrected her. "Moral turpitude."

Brenda grinned. "I thought that was the stuff you used to take paint off."

Joe laughed too, and Nichols fumed some more.

He pointed at them again. "Will you two get serious? You have to keep your mouths shut about everything you've heard here."

"Oh, grow up. We're more interested in the thieving going on in this place, and who murdered that poor woman in the ladies earlier tonight. But I'll tell you this, if this person you're protecting turns up in the middle of our enquiries, you'll need a damn sight more than MI5 to shut us up. I don't care what the bigwigs from Westminster get up to, but I don't hold with theft... or murder."

Nichols glowered. "You have my personal assurance that this person had nothing to do with Renata Chappell's death."

Joe fought back. "If you know that, it means that you murdered her."

Chapter Twelve

By the time the fingerprint forensic people were finished, and Joe and Brenda had tidied up their chalet, it was half past one in the morning. As arranged, they shared a bed, but it was all they shared. The moment Brenda's head hit the pillow, she was asleep, and Joe was not far behind her.

A call from Sheila to Brenda's smartphone at half past eight woke them both.

"Do you know what time it is?" Brenda complained. "And do you know what time we got to bed at?"

"Serves you right," Sheila replied. "You should go to bed to sleep, not play games."

"For your information—"

Sheila cut Brenda off. "I don't want any of the gory details. I've been up since seven, and I have some information. There's a café just along the road from the boarding house where I'm staying. Edie's Eatery. It's easy to spot. It's the only place on the road. How about we meet there half past nine?"

"We'll be there… If you're lucky."

Brenda killed the call and passed the message to Joe, who rolled out of bed with a groan and made his way to the bathroom.

Breaking the habit of a lifetime, he skipped his morning shave, and five minutes later, Brenda entered the bathroom while Joe dressed for the day.

Outside, the sky was clear and the temperature was already in the low twenties. It would be another sweltering day, but it had its advantages in that he could wear shorts and a T-shirt, which, if nothing else, would keep the Edströms and their members quiet.

Brenda emerged from the bathroom similarly dressed, wearing a pair of white shorts and a white, cotton top with capped sleeves.

"She didn't say what the information was?" Joe asked as they stepped out of the chalet and he unlocked his car.

"She didn't have time. I'm absolutely jiggered, Joe. I needed at least another two hours' sleep."

"Join the club. We'll just have to try and catch up this afternoon."

Settling into the car, he started the engine and pulled slowly out of their parking space, turning right towards the exit several hundred yards away. Almost immediately, Håkan appeared from the rear of reception, naked as the day he was born, and flagged them down.

Letting the window down, Joe averted his eyes and Håkan leaned in. "The police have been here all night, Mr Murray. Are you any further forward with your deliberations on the thefts?"

"No. They've taken our fingerprints for elimination, and then it's all about what Kirsty Hinch can come up with from the video she took away. Right now, we have to meet our colleague, Mrs Riley, in Skegness. Apparently, she has some information for us. Beyond that, Håkan, I can't tell you anything. When we get back from seeing Sheila, I'll catch up with you and bring you up to speed." He scowled. "And it would help, if you put some clothes on."

"It would be a lot more to the point if you took yours off." And with that, Håkan turned away and walked back to reception.

Moving off, Joe made his feelings plain. "This place is beginning to get on my wick."

"Too many wicks for me to get on, and it's not often you'll hear me say something like that." She cackled. "And talking about wicks—"

"No. Don't. Please. Not this early in the morning."

With the windows open, the fresh air invigorated them, and they both relaxed, savouring the breeze ruffling their hair, cooling their skin as they drove along.

As Sheila had promised, Edie's Eatery was easy to find, especially with their friend's Fiat parked outside. Joe slotted his ageing Vauxhall in behind her newer, smarter, little car, and they entered the café to find it about half full.

"The Lazy Luncheonette would be chocabloc at this hour," Joe muttered.

"No it wouldn't," Brenda replied as they joined Sheila. "It's just gone half past nine, and the draymen would be gone along with all the office wallahs." She smiled at her best friend. "Good morning, Sheila. And how are you?"

Sheila studied them both. "A lot fitter than you two look, I guess. I've told you before, you're getting too much exercise for people of your age."

His eyes on the menu, Joe said, "You're right. It's a hell of a job tidying the chalet up at one o'clock in the morning." He beamed up as a middle-aged proprietor came to the table, notebook in hand. "I'll have a full English, please. What about you two?"

"I've already eaten," Sheila reminded them. "I'll just have another cup of tea, please."

"And I think I'll join Joe with a full English breakfast," Brenda said.

Edie (that was who they assumed the woman to be) took their order, and returned to the counter.

"So, what have you got for us, Sheila?"

It was Joe posing the question, and Sheila reached into her bag to retrieve her iPad.

"With regard to Welsby, Simpson, Kesteven, Ormond and Pollitt, I learned nothing more, but there are two other anomalies: Diane Randleson and Renata Chappell."

"Well, Renata's bound to be the odd one out, isn't she?" Brenda hurried on to answer her rhetorical question. "She's dead, and all the others are still alive, including Diane Randleson."

Sheila frowned her disapproval. "They also have no history. When I checked up on the membership, I could backtrack on quite a lot of them. Many are business people with genuine, naturist convictions, and they make no bones about it on various social media sites. Kesteven is an academic and Ormond is an American. Welsby has his own business which he runs with Simpson, and Pollitt, as I suggested sells odds and sods online. The odd ones out are Diane and Renata interestingly. No social media accounts, no history whatsoever, nothing from Companies House, so they're not registered as directors with any company or organisation. In fact, I couldn't find anything out about either of them. Most of the other members are fairly easy to track down, even if few of them are actually married. Neil Kesteven and Gina Ormond are partners, so, too, are William Welsby and Arabella Simpson. Do people not believe in marriage anymore?"

"Well, I certainly don't," Joe said as Edie returned with fresh tea for them all. "It's far too expensive."

Edie looked down her nose at him. "I think you'll find, sir, that we're quite competitive."

"No, sorry, missus. I wasn't talking about your prices. I was talking about the cost of marriage."

"Hmm. You sound like my old man."

Joe smiled at his two companions. "There you are. I rest my case." While Edie went away, Joe focused on Sheila. "I take your point, Sheila, but you may be reading too much into this. Not everyone is into social media. I'm not. All right, so The Lazy Luncheonette has a Facebook Page and a Twitter account, but it's Lee, Cheryl and Kayleigh who keep it up-to-date. I don't have anything to do with it. As for Companies House, well, just because they're not involved with any large concern, doesn't mean much. Think about…" He allowed his mind to meander for a moment. "Les Tanner. He doesn't do social media, and he's not the director of any company. He's just a pain in the backside, departmental manager at Sanford Borough Council. So if you ran a similar search on Les, you get the same results."

"With the possible exception that you wouldn't find Les and Sylvia swanning around in the altogether at Sun Kissed," Brenda said.

Sheila conceded Joe's point. "All I'm saying is, they

appear to be out of step with every other member."

The food arrived. Joe and Brenda tucked into a well cooked, perfectly presented full English breakfast, both of them eating with gusto, as if they had not been fed for several days.

"I assume you will be sticking the cost of this on Håkan Edström's bill," Brenda commented as she swallowed a large piece of Lincolnshire sausage.

"Damn right I will."

"That's a bit unfair, Joe," Sheila observed. "Wherever you are, you have to eat breakfast."

"Quite right, but I didn't notice him let us eat for free in the dining room last night." Having wolfed down the food, Joe pushed his empty plate away and helped himself to a second cup of tea. "Did you turn up anything in your researches on criminal convictions?"

"Nothing."

"What about the staff?" Brenda asked. "That Ellis and the young woman who works with him behind the bar. What's her name? Olga?"

"Olga Dellon," Sheila reported, "and neither of them have any criminal record as far as I can ascertain, but remember I can only check on local newspapers. You really need to speak to Kirsty Hinch about this. If any of the members or the staff have crossed swords with the law, she'll know."

"Yes but she'll be up to her neck in this murder inquiry. Talking of which, it's all very well you pointing the finger at Diane Randleson, but we know for a fact it can't have been her. She was in full view of us when Renata Chappell was murdered."

"Assuming we know what time Renata was murdered. You say the body was still warm, Joe, but like Kirsty told us, getting an accurate time of death is quite often nothing more than intelligent guesswork."

Joe bowed to her superior logic. "All I'm saying is it's unlikely to be her."

Breakfast over, Joe paid the bill, and they ambled out into the rising heat of the day. By mutual agreement, they decided to spend a little time on the seafront, and while Brenda climbed into Sheila's car, Joe pulled out ahead of them and led the way to the promenade and the car park close to the concentration of amenities near the funfair. Once parked up, Brenda bought ice cream for all three, and they found a seat overlooking the beach.

There was not a breath of wind, and as if to comment upon it, the huge windfarm set out to sea, showed no activity, all turbines stopped. It was a little after 10 o'clock, and already the beach was busy with families, children playing in the sand, parents trying to catch some sleep, and to their right, a line of donkeys ready to take riders on a circular tour on that side of the beach. From the fairground came the usual cacophony of mixed music as one or other ride got under way, and for all three it brought a sense of peace.

"Remember the last time we were here," Brenda said. "Early New Year, absolutely hammering down and freezing cold."

"We went to Mablethorpe on the Saturday," Sheila reminded them. "And Joe was playing detective. Again."

"And Brenda got her shoes stuck in the sand," Joe commented. "I had to rescue her and her shoes."

"Some things never change," Brenda agreed with her friend. "Oh, Joe, while we're talking about Skegness, you do know that Sheila and I are going to Cyprus for a week in about a month's time. When you get back from servicing Alison's requirements in Tenerife."

He ignored her final remark. "You keep reminding me. The only thing I can't work out is what does Cyprus have to do with Skegness?"

"You won't be with us," Sheila said. "Which probably means there won't be a murder."

Joe finished his ice cream. "Wouldn't be much point going in that case."

More minutes of silence followed. They watched the antics of people on the beach and wallowed in the nostalgia of a typical, British seaside scene on a sunny, summer Saturday.

Sheila broke into their contemplation. "What are you two up to now?"

"Back to Sun Kissed," Joe said. "You're not coming with us?"

"I thought I made my feelings clear on that matter, Joe. I find that place more than uncomfortable. I will join you for dinner tonight, but the minute the meal's over, I'll go back to my digs. And naturally if I come across anything you need to know in the meantime, I'll ring."

In an effort to encourage her, Brenda said, "It's not as bad as you think, Sheila. You have to learn to, oh, I don't know, edit out the nudity."

"A bit difficult considering it's staring you in the face everywhere you turn," was Sheila's tart response.

Brenda considered it. "Tell you what. You go back to Sun Kissed, Joe, and I'll hang out in Skegness with Sheila."

"Oh, great. Leave me to deal with all the skin. I thought we were supposed to be a team."

"We could all stay here," Sheila suggested. "With this poor woman's murder, we probably won't get any further forward on the park, so I don't think Håkan will miss us."

"I am not spending the day shopping with you two in Skeggy."

Brenda grinned "We're furthering inquiries, Joe. Cos, we will check out the secondhand shops. Won't we, Sheila?"

"Of course we will."

"Gar. Don't give me that. You'll come back to Sun Kissed loaded with shopping bags. I know you too well."

Sheila glanced at her watch. "Whatever we decide, it's getting on for eleven o'clock, and time we were making a move."

They ambled slowly back to the car park, and when they got there, Joe was not entirely surprised to see Carol Liddle parked close to them, obviously waiting for them to return.

"Which one of you loudmouths told the cops who I was?"

Joe squared up to her. "It's good to see you too, Ms Liddle. How did you enjoy your night in the cells? Comfortable was it? Did they bring you breakfast in bed?"

"I'll crucify you. All of you. Keep your eyes on next Sunday's tabloids. You will be mincemeat."

Joe reacted in kind. "Why don't you shut your trap, and try listening up for once? I don't know who Nichols works for these days, but he's obviously well-connected, and whoever told the filth that you were a reporter is irrelevant. Work it out, woman. Between the time that body turned up in the ladies, and the time Nichols arrived, someone made a phone call. Someone higher up. Someone important in Whitehall or Westminster. It was nothing to do with us. And where Kirsty Hinch is concerned, she needed to know who you were, because the minute she checked up and found there was no such person as Doctor Delia Coll, you would have been knee deep in it and sinking further." He paused to let the lesson sink in. "It might help, if you told us exactly who you were looking at."

"I can't. It comes under the Official Secrets Act, and if I say one word to you or anyone else, I'm looking at twenty years."

"Yes, well, think about this. You say one word about me, Sheila, Brenda, any of us in that cheap rag, and you'll be looking at a massive bill for libel. If you're looking for a story, why don't you try the old slag heaps in Sanford?"

Carol perked up. "Why? What's going on with them?"

"Nothing, but if you dig up the grass, you'll find plenty of dirt underneath."

Chapter Thirteen

Joe watched Sheila and Brenda drive away, and with a final glare at Carol Liddle, pulled out of the car park himself, but instead of following the road back to Sun Kissed, he turned north along the promenade, and working on memories of the last time they were in Skegness found his way to Park Road, where he turned into the public car park of the police station.

He presented himself at reception and asked for Kirsty Hinch. She appeared a few minutes later, and escorted him through to her small office.

"Not much I can tell you about the dead woman, Joe. She's proving difficult to track down. I don't know whether Nichols knows anything, but if he does, he's keeping it to himself." She tutted. "Bloody secret service."

"I thought he was still a cop."

"He is, but the people he works for are allied to the intelligence services."

Joe laughed. "I've just seen Carol Liddle on the main car park by the beach and she's moaning she's had to shut up because of the Official Secrets Act." He pulled himself together. "Anyway, that's not why I'm here. Murder annoys me and I know you said it probably has nothing to do with the thieving, I disagree. The timing of the murder was a damn sight too opportune for my liking."

He went on to outline his thinking and Kirsty listened before pausing to think it through, and then responding. "Possible, I suppose, but as I said last night, Joe, there's absolutely no evidence to back that up, and the search of Renata Chappell's chalet turned up no stolen goods... or at least, nothing on the list of latest thefts Edström gave to us. And she's not what you could call a regular at Sun Kissed. If

I remember rightly, this was her first time."

Joe accepted her verdict. "If I do turn up anything, I'll let you know, but I'm more interested in the thieving, and there are a few people we're looking at." He dug into his pockets and took out his handwritten list which he passed to her.

Kirsty spent a moment or two studying it before commenting. "I can tell you now that Kesteven is a respected academic. He's unlikely to be involved in either the thieving or the murder. I will run a check on the other names."

"Thanks, Kirsty, and like I said, if I come across anything, I'll bell you. Oh, while I think on, the members of staff on that list. There are two we can't get a hook on. Well, we can, but they're snow white and we wondered if they had any criminal form."

"You're looking at staff too?"

"As much as the members. Maybe more so. I mean, it makes sense when you think about it. Where would a naturist hide the loot?"

Kirsty laughed. "I can think of one or two places for the small stuff."

"Yeah, but you'd notice him walking odd if he jammed the laptop—"

"Yes, Joe. You don't have to spell it out. Anyway, we're running checks on the members as it is, and I can add these two to the list if they're not already on it." She studied the list. "I don't have to check on Allyn. He has form. Mostly for fighting, drunk and disorderly. I wouldn't put it past him to get a little light-fingered, but he'd be running the risk of losing his job and his freedom. Can't say I've heard of the woman." Kirsty made a note. "I'll get Brightwood to run them through the database and see what comes up. I'll either ring or text you the results. Okay?"

"That's what I like. A public servant being of service."

"Yeah, well, if and when we get through all this, mine's a voddy and tonic."

Joe came out into the hot day again and before he got into his car, he was sweating. A lack of forethought had seen him park the vehicle facing straight into the sun and when he climbed behind the wheel he could hardly breathe. Worse, when he put his hand on the steering wheel, he felt like it would burn the skin off.

"You're an idiot, Joe Murray," he told himself and let both windows down. Not that it did any good. There was no wind to bring any relief. Not until he started the engine and moved off.

Circling the roundabout where the unique and well-known clock tower stood, he glanced to his right and along Lumley Road, the main shopping thoroughfare, and he knew that no matter what Sheila and Brenda promised regarding a check on the second-hand shops, they would be indulging in their favourite pastime, shopping, or retail therapy as they described it.

If Joe's response to Brenda's insistence on staying with Sheila for the afternoon had been muted it was because he felt he understood. The three had been close friends for the better part of half a century, and the two women, both widowed, Sheila with a short but shocking second marriage behind her, were all but inseparable. Joe would not cast himself in the role of most important man in their lives, but he knew he was high up the list. Despite the ribbing, the teasing, he was one in whom they had implicit trust, and he felt the same way about them. As a trio, they were akin to Dumas' musketeers and except in rare, unavoidable circumstances, they would always be there for one another. Hadn't they dragged him off to Torremolinos after his faux heart attack a couple of years back? Hadn't they fought for his freedom when he was thrown in jail, suspected of murder? And hadn't Joe, the worst scrapper in the world, thrown himself at the evil man ready to kill Sheila, confronted the hardened criminal threatening Brenda?

In the case of Sun Kissed Holiday Park, while Brenda appeared to be handling the naturism better than either Joe or Sheila, he guessed it still disturbed her. She had a much freer attitude to life and love than either of her companions, a facet of her character which led to unwarranted allegations of 'loose-leggedness' to coin a Yorkshire-ism. It was not true, but she was not as fazed by nudity as perhaps Joe and certainly not as much as was Sheila. And yet, for all that she covered it with her customary humour, he believed that shopping with Sheila was one way of escaping the amount of bare flesh on display because deep down, it did disturb her. It was too far out of her comfort zones.

For his part, Joe could not criticise or condemn Sun Kissed nor it members for their lifestyle choice, but if he'd been aware of it the previous Monday, he would have turned Edström down flat. And there was no one to blame for the situation other than himself. He should have shut up long enough to listen to Edström.

It was too late to worry about it, he thought as he turned into the holiday park. An agreement was an agreement, and like it or not, uncomfortable or otherwise, he would have to see it through. Besides, there was a murder to be solved as well as the routine thefts, and murder, the taking of another's life, always brought out the determined sleuth in him.

Once parked behind the chalet, his first port of call was reception. Ambling through the pool area, his eyes everywhere but on the naked bodies around him, he called first at the bar where he sank a half of lager, and then made his way to the office where Margot answered his ring on the bell.

"I do wish you people would cover yourselves up," he grumbled, purposely avoiding the sight of her pendulous and unfettered bosom waving in front of him.

"You should be used to it by now, Mr Murray. What do you want?"

"A word with either you, Håkan, or both of you."

"Come through." She lifted the flap and led him into the office, where Håkan was working on the computer.

"Ah, my friend. You have news for us?"

"No. Not so you'd notice, but I do have some questions concerning your bar staff, Allyn and Dellon."

A frown creased Håkan's brow. "Ellis and Olga? What about them?"

"How long have you known them?"

It was Margot who answered. "This is Ellis's second season. He was here last year as a barman-stroke-waiter but when our manager retired last year, we promoted him. He's good at his job, works long hours – don't we all – and we have no problems with him."

"And what about Ms Dellon?"

"She was personal friend of Ellis's," Håkan replied. "He recommended her, we interviewed her, she has the relevant experience and good references, so we took her on."

"Do they live on site?"

"No. We don't have room for them. Mr Murray, Joe, I don't know where your thinking is going, but we have absolute trust in them. They live at different addresses and if there is any liaison between them, it's no concern of ours... or yours."

"It is if they're your thieves. Especially with them living off site. For all you know, one of those two addresses could be an Aladdin's cave of knocked off goodies... including my laptop."

"I don't believe it," Margot declared.

"Your choice, but you hired me, remember. You're paying the bill and to do a proper job, I have to consider all possibilities. On a possibly unrelated matter, what do you know about Diane Randleson and her dead pal, Renata Chappell."

"No more than we know about our other members, which amounts to very little, and your narrow-minded friend, Mrs Riley, has all that information."

Joe rankled at the description of Sheila. "She's not narrow-minded. She's just uncomfortable. Every bit as uncomfortable as I am. Getting back to Randleson, do you know what she does for a living?"

"A civil servant, I believe," Margot said. "Again, your friend, Mrs Riley, has the necessary information, and the files which you had are missing."

"Yeah, well, I made the mistake of stepping out of the chalet last night to feed myself, and that gave our opportunist thief the gap he was looking for. But don't worry, Margot. I'll have him." In the light of her thinly veiled accusation, Joe's irritation began to get the better of him and he rose, but as he prepared to leave, he paused. "Diane Randleson. What chalet is she in?"

"Number fourteen," Håkan replied. "She was in number twelve, but we had to move her at the insistence of the police. Fourteen is almost directly opposite yours."

Joe left reception and to avoid the nudity, took the rear track back to his chalet. Once inside, he filled and switched on the kettle, then parted the front blinds about twelve inches, so he could look straight across at chalet #14. Across there, the blinds were fully closed and he recalled Ms Randleson's insistence that she would not parade naked. And yet when he and Håkan spoke to her shortly after the discovery of Renata Chappell's body, she insisted that she was a frequent visitor to naturist sites. He also recalled Sheila's information that Randleson had turned up at Sun Kissed every week for the last god knows how many weeks.

Was it possible that she had disguised herself as a man and broken into their chalet the previous night? He made an effort to recall her body shape. Tall, slender, but with a fulsome bosom. She fitted the height criteria, and given the poor lighting, it would be just about possible.

But when? According to his memory, she had not left the bar after showing up with Carol Liddle. A more important question was why? Was she the serial thief who had been at work on the site ever since the season began to pick up? Or was she concerned that Joe, Sheila, Brenda held information which might implicate her in the murder of her chalet mate?

As he watched, Diane's door opened, and Vivienne Foulkes stepped out accompanied by a man whom Joe recognised as Peter Brandon.

Odd. Although they were about the same age, both of them something like ten years older than Diane, there was no mention in Sheila's research to identify them as a couple, and yet they walked from chalet #14 along the side of the pool, and disappeared into another chalet further down.

The truth of the situation, or at least a better than working theory, occurred to Joe right away. He snatched up his smartphone, and rang Sheila. No answer. He did not need many guesses to work out that she and Brenda were in a clothing shop, probably trying on various items of apparel in the changing cubicles, a situation in which neither of them would answer the phone.

The connection went to voicemail, and he left a message asking her to ring back the moment she was free.

It was less than ten minutes when she called him back. "What do you want, Joe? We're very busy."

"Oh yes? Primark? Dorothy Perkins? Or have you gone upmarket in Debenhams?"

"Where we are is none of your business. What do you want?"

"Vivienne Foulkes and Peter Brandon. I'm working off the top of my head, but I don't think you indicated any relationship between them."

"As far as my researches go, there isn't any, as you would know if you read the files."

"Bit difficult considering my laptop's been nicked along with the original files Håkan gave us."

"Oh. Sorry. I forgot. And of course, we didn't go into those kind of details last night, did we? We'll be stopping for lunch soon, and I'll check up and get back to you."

Joe ended the call, and drank his tea. There was little more to be done until Sheila came back to him, and if skiving off, shopping in Skegness was good enough for them, then much the same argument applied to him, so he took himself to the bedroom, kicked off his shoes, lay down on top of bed, closed his eyes, and drifted off to catch up with some much needed sleep.

Chapter Fourteen

It was almost two o'clock when Sheila rang again, and the news was as puzzling as ever.

"I haven't been able to learn much about either of them, Joe, but they are not together. According to the information Sun Kissed have on them, they don't even come from the same area. Mrs Foulkes is from somewhere near Scunthorpe, North Lincolnshire and Peter Brandon is from Spalding, South Lincolnshire."

"Regular visitors?" Joe asked.

"Here for two weeks only," Sheila reported, "and they're not sharing a chalet."

Joe chewed his lip. "Coincidence. The same two weeks that Diane Randleson who normally only comes for weekends, is here. I put something across to Kirsty earlier. Where would a naturist stash the loot?"

There was a brief hiatus while Sheila passed the comment on, and Joe could hear Brenda howling with laughter in the background.

"Where are you?" Joe demanded.

"In a pub called The Tipsy Cow."

"That sounds perfect for Brenda from the way she's laughing."

"Be thankful she can't hear you saying that. Now what were you saying about a naturist hiding the loot?"

"Okay. It's an obvious question, isn't it? But think about it this way, Diane Randleson refuses to parade naked. Is that because her pants are full of cash and jewellery and stuff? And just in case suspicion should ever fall on her, she'd need a couple of accomplices or even fences where she could shift the stuff against the danger of someone – the filth – searching her room."

"Ah. You're thinking Vivienne Foulkes and Peter Brandon. But I just told you, Joe, they live at least seventy miles apart."

"You mean they live seventy miles apart according to the information they've given Sun Kissed. Besides even if it's true, what difference does it make? They could have worked together in, say, London years ago. I would never have given them a thought, but after what I saw earlier, they're in the frame. I could do with Brenda back here to help me hassle Diane."

There was another brief pause before Sheila reported, "I doubt that she'll be much use. She's already sunk a couple of Camparis. And before you ask, I've made my position clear. I will have nothing to do with that place, even to help you question Diane Randleson."

"No worries. Leave it all to Joe. Just be ready to bail me out when she has me arrested for harassment."

They ended the call on a promise from Sheila to bring Brenda back to the chalet by five o'clock. Joe rolled a cigarette, and stepped out to the rear of the chalet, where the view, restricted by heavy woodland, was nevertheless preferable to the disturbing sights out front.

And while he stood, enjoying the bite of tobacco on his damaged lungs, he ran a series of questions through his mind.

Diane could not possibly be guilty of Renata's murder. She had the best alibi possible: Joe and his two friends. Also, if she really was the thief, why hadn't she gone home this morning? Sun Kissed had been swarming with police all night, and the danger of exposure, being caught with the goods, was too great to risk. On the other hand, if Vivienne Foulkes and Peter Brandon were working with her, Diane would not be in possession of any of the stolen property, and the law had no cause to search their chalet(s). Turning the argument on its head, Joe reasoned that if either of the two supposed fences were caught in possession, they would not hesitate to take Diane with them, so perhaps it was a more logical approach to stay where they were for the coming week. With the murder of her chalet mate, Diane would have a reasonable excuse for getting away from the park. Vivienne and Brandon had none, and for them to fly the coop would arouse suspicion which in turn, might well fall back upon Diane.

As he puffed contentedly on his cigarette, another angle occurred to him. After last night's events, it was entirely possible that Vivienne and Brandon had already disposed of the gains (including Joe's laptop) and that might explain why they called upon Diane. To divide the spoils and draw up a makeshift plan for the coming days, one which would see them basking in all their angelic – and naked – innocence.

He tossed a cigarette to the ground, and crushed it underfoot, returned to the kitchen, and made himself fresh tea as more questions bombarded him.

Why a naturist site? In Diane's case it as not just one but several, if the woman was to be believed. In terms of burglary, theft, a site where clothing was optional yet discouraged was one of the worst places to use as a base.

Once again, Joe turned the conclusion on its head. Perhaps Sun Kissed and its ilk were chosen precisely because they were the worst kind of holiday park to ply their dubious trade. In other words, who would expect to encounter professional burglars, people accustomed to deploying heavy disguises, on such a site?

With the time coming up to half past three in the afternoon, he reached his reluctant conclusion. Diane Randleson would have to be questioned, and it would need delicate handling. If he had it all wrong, the outcome would be anyone's guess. At the very least, Joe could foresee him, Brenda, and Sheila thrown out of the park, the contract with the Edströms torn up. And beyond that, if Diane chose to prosecute for slander, it could cost them a lot of money.

Finishing his second cup of tea, he decided it was time to bite the bullet. Wearing only his shorts and T-shirt, he stepped out of the front, circled the pool area, and rapped on the door of chalet #14.

Indulging his aversion to the flesh on show, he kept his face turned to the door, but a movement in the corner of his left eye drew his attention. The blinds were closed, but when he glanced in that direction, they parted a couple of inches, and Diane's face appeared in the gap. Joe beamed a crooked smile and mouthed, "I need a word." Diane held up two fingers, a gesture which might have caused Joe to take offence to were it not for her nodding in agreement, allowing him to translate the two fingers as 'two minutes'.

While he waited, he glanced at his right, further down the line of chalets, in time to see Peter Brandon appear from whatever number he and Vivienne Foulkes had disappeared into. Joe charitably assumed that they'd been getting down to nature in more ways than one, but when Brandon saw him, he changed his mind, and stepped back into the chalet.

It could have been pure coincidence, but Joe was certain that Brandon looked straight at him before deciding to duck out of sight. Joe's suspicion-ometer rose several points.

The door of #14 opened, and Diane, wearing her familiar bikini, stood back to let him in, and closed the door behind him.

From the off she looked uncomfortable, and for the first time, Joe realised what a risk he was taking. This woman had not murdered Renata Chappell, but if her associates, Foulkes and Brandon were the guilty parties, Joe could well be next on their list. That went double having noticed Brandon's suspicious behaviour.

Diane invited him to sit at the table, and took the chair opposite. "What can I do for you, Mr Murray? If it's about Renata's murder, I can't tell you any more than I did last night." She shuffled in her seat and once more appeared as if she were in some discomfort. As if she had an unpleasant task to perform.

Joe put aside worries for his safety and breezed into the conversation. "That's fine, Diane – you don't mind if I call you Diane, do you?"

"Of course not."

She shuffled in her seat and made a barely concealed effort to adjust the lower half of her bikini, and the truth dawned on Joe.

This woman point blank refused to parade naked, yet had no problem with nudity in private. It was obvious that she had been in the altogether when Joe knocked on the door and had to put the bikini on in a hurry.

He relaxed. His safety was not (yet) compromised, and anyway enough people must have seen him knocking on the door to guarantee his security for the time being.

"I'm Joe, by the way."

He paused a moment, deliberately looked around the chalet, trying to give the impression that he was marshalling his thoughts, when in fact he was looking for any sign of stolen goods. There was nothing of any significance other than a small, glass jar of some dark orange substance on the unit under the television, and whatever it was (he guessed it might be marmalade) Joe could not see it being part of a robbery haul.

With nothing else apparent (did he expect there to be?) he focused on the woman again. "I've investigated any number of murders, Diane, and even though you can't tell us anything about what happened last night, you never know what information you might have concerning Renata and possible suspects. Now, I did ask you whether she had any enemies. Let me ask you again. Has she got into any arguments since your arrival here at Sun Kissed?"

"Not that I'm aware of. And by and large, Mr Murray, we kept ourselves to ourselves. It's not that we're particularly shy, but we believe in privacy. It's why I was hesitant to answer some of your questions last night. Frankly, any relationship I had with Renata is no business of yours nor the police."

Despite Diane's denial the previous evening, Joe took her response as an indication that theirs was a same-sex arrangement. Again, the conclusion was irrelevant to Sheila's concerns. "I understand you're a civil servant. Do you mind my asking what department you work for?"

Joe did not even know why he posed the question, if not for small talk, but he was surprised by Diane's response.

"I do mind. Well, it's not me that minds, it's Whitehall as

an institution. I suppose in your day-to-day life you've come across many civil servants, and while most of them will identify themselves if calling on business, in private they are reluctant to go into details of their department or their work. Imagine, for example, that I worked for the Benefits Agency. Here we are meeting on a naturist site, you learn of my free-time commitment to a more natural lifestyle, you know of my department, and the next thing I know, you're pressuring me to show you how your benefits can be, er, fiddled. Let's use the term."

"And let's use the term blackmail," Joe said. "It is more accurate."

"There you are then. You understand exactly what I mean. For that reason, I prefer not to say what government department I work for." Diane looked uncomfortable yet again, and stood up. "Would you excuse me for a moment? I need to visit the bathroom."

Joe nodded. "When you gotta go, you gotta go."

With Diane out of the room, Joe took a hasty tour of the chalet and kitchen. He found nothing. On returning to the living area, he picked up the jar he had seen beneath the television. It was not marmalade but make up. Probably belonging to Renata. He read the label. *Ben Nye Media Pro HD Concealer* in burnt orange. Wasn't that the stuff they used to create a fake tan? His opinion of Diane and Renata Chappell dropped several points. Posers. The pair of them. Determined to look the part.

The sound of Diane making her way back from the bathroom made him put the jar back and scurry to his seat at the table.

"I'm sorry about that."

"Like I said, it's no problem."

She went on. "As I was saying, it's enough for you to know that I am an ordinary civil servant in an unspecified department. I don't actually work in Whitehall, but no matter where we're based, we're a reticent breed by nature."

"Fine. No problem. I think I understand where you're coming from, and I'm through anyway. If you can't tell me anything about Renata or throw any light on the persistent thefts on this site, I don't think I've anything more to ask you."

Delivering the words 'throw any light on the persistent thefts' Joe studied her face, but as always, it betrayed no emotion. He stood and made for the door, Diane followed him, and as she opened the door, Joe stopped and faced her.

"Oh. I noticed Vivienne Foulkes and Peter Brandon called on you earlier. Friends, are you?"

"Nothing of the kind. They came to offer their condolences on Renata's death."

"Right. I see. Sorry if I sound nosy, but it goes with the private eye territory. I don't think I'll need to bother you again. Thanks for your help."

As he was about to step outside, she ran a finger down the right hand side of her face, and the action caused Joe's suspicions to rise. It was an action he was perfectly familiar with but coming from…

He brought his thoughts under control and considered his next move.

He had intended making his way along the chalet lines and finding the one harbouring Vivienne Foulkes of Peter Brandon, but his febrile mind began to put together thin strands of loose information, pointers he would need more information on, and that information was currently several miles away, shopping in Skegness.

He made his way first to the bar, where Olga Dellon served him with a half of lager, which he took to a vacant table in the far corner, adjacent to Ignatius Isherwood. In need of thinking time, he had intended to sit and enjoy a quiet drink while he mulled over what he had just witnessed. Aye-Aye had other ideas.

Like so many others fellow naturist, the old man wore nothing at all, and again in common with other members, was not at all fazed by Joe's light clothing. But he was irritated at the revelations of the previous night.

"So you and your harem are a set of perishing snoops, are you?"

"We did say so yesterday afternoon if you remember," Joe retorted. "It could be worse. We could be reporters."

"She was, wasn't she? That so-called doctor. No wonder she turned me down when I tried to pull her."

Joe almost laughed at the thought of Aye-Aye trying to seduce Carol Liddle. "Don't take it personally. We know her of old, and if you pulled her, you'd find yourself in the centre pages of some downmarket rag next Sunday."

"So what are you doing now? Chasing up that little tramp who was topped? See if you can crack that as well as the thieving."

It was a curious question, not so much the old man's assumption, but his description of Renata Chappell. "Tramp?"

"Seen her before," Aye-Aye commented. "She's been here a time or two with that other tart, Diane whatever she calls herself."

Not according to Håkan Edström she hadn't. Joe put the thought to one side. "Just to put you right, we have nothing to do with Renata Chappell's murder. As we said, we were hired to identify the burglar."

"Ah. About bloody time, too. Thieving toerag got away with my old navy watch. Valuable piece of kit, that. Had it since I was a midshipman when I came out of Britannia." He grunted again. "Before your time, I'd guess."

Joe guessed Aye-Aye's age at about seventy. "I'm older than you think. Do me a favour, describe this watch. You never know. We might yet get a trace on it."

"Can't be bothered. Sentimental value only. Whoever took it would be lucky to get ten shillings for it."

An idea occurred to Joe. "You sound as if you've hit on most of the women here, what about Vivienne Foulkes? Or is she too busy with Peter Brandon?"

"Couple of middle aged rockers, they are."

"So am I."

"There you are then. You know the score. You should do with two dollies hanging on your arm."

At that moment, Ellis Allyn made his rounds collecting

glasses, and making no effort to lower his voice, spoke to Joe, "I told you about him, didn't I? He's a daft old sod. Just take no notice of him."

Aye-Aye took instant umbrage. "In my day I'd have had you horsewhipped for that kind of comment."

"Yes, and if the tales I've heard are to be believed, you'd have wanted Olga to lay the whip on you after you're done with me."

Chapter Fifteen

Despite considering Ignatius Isherwood to be sex obsessed and quite dotty, Joe took his views back to the chalet. His final remark on Vivienne Foulkes and Peter Brandon, 'a couple of old rockers' confirmed what Joe suspected. Different addresses, different parts of the country or whatever they claimed, they were a pair. Whether that meant life or business partners, remained to be seen, and if his slight suspicion of Diane Randleson was confirmed, then he understood so much more about what had gone on the previous evening. The only question left to be answered was when Diane had carried out the raid on Joe's chalet, but he realised there was enough confusion after the discovery of Renata's body to allow a suitable opportunity.

It was coming up to four o'clock. He took out his smartphone and rang Sheila.

"Yes, Joe, we'll be back shortly."

"No. Stay where you are. I need to come into Skegness to find something out. Where exactly are you?"

"In the Hildreds shopping centre. It's at the junction where Lumley Road splits from the High Street. There's a little coffee shop just inside. It's not difficult to find."

"Stay put. I'll be with you in twenty minutes."

"Yes, Joe, but if you think we're going to sit here for the next half-hour waiting for you, you've another think coming. When you get here give us a call."

As he climbed into his car, drove to the exit, and turned back towards Skegness, Sheila's last words puzzled him. He'd known these women for half a century and there was no way they would finish coffee and cakes in less than twenty minutes, or even half an hour as Sheila suggested.

This late on a Friday afternoon, the traffic was building up, and Sheila's estimate was nearer the mark. It was all of twenty-five minutes before Joe slotted his car into one of the few remaining spaces on the parking area behind the shopping mall and paid the fee.

Even with time coming up to half past four, the place was packed, but he eventually found Sheila right where she said they would be, seated outside a small coffee shop. She had a look of severe disapproval on her face, and it did not take much metal effort to work out why. Alongside her, Brenda lolled in her seat, her eyes glazed and a stupid smile spread across her face.

"Drunk?"

It was a pointless question as Sheila confirmed. "She downed four Camparis over lunch in The Tipsy Cow. I tried to warn her, but you know what it's like talking to her when she's in that frame of mind."

Joe nodded. "A waste of breath. Damn. I needed her something like sober, too."

Sheila frowned. "Needed her sober? Joe, it's not up to me to disapprove of whatever you and Brenda get up to, but—"

He cut her off. "You're getting as bad as Brenda for jumping to the wrong conclusions. It's too complicated to explain right now, and I'm not exactly sure of my footing." He dipped into his wallet and threw a fiver on the table. "Get her another black coffee and order for us, too. I just need to nip into Superdrug. I won't be long."

"Superdrug? What could you possibly want from…"

Joe did not hear the rest of Sheila's obvious question. He was already on his way into the store.

Once inside he studied the range of make-up and cosmetics available, and feeling completely out of the depth opened the web browser on his phone, and looked up the jar of foundation cream he'd seen in Diane's chalet.

With a suitable image, he approached a member of staff and showed it to her. "Do you stock this or something very like it?"

The young woman looked at the image, then at Joe,

suspicion haunted her brown eyes.

Joe realised at once what was going through her mind and hurried on to explain. "It's not for me. It's for my missus. She's always doing it. Sending me for this kind of stuff when I don't really know what I'm talking about."

It was difficult to judge from the assistant's face whether she believed him or not, but she readily explained. "I don't think we stock that particular brand, but we do have similar products, usually in a tube or a stick."

Joe gave up. "Okay. Sorry, but it's no use to me. She specified a jar. Any ideas where I might get one?"

"To be honest, that looks more like theatrical make-up, and I can't think of anywhere in Skegness where you might find it. You could order online."

"I could, but they're not likely to deliver this evening, are they? Thanks for your help."

He came out of the shop and Googled 'theatrical supplies, Skegness' only to come up with a plethora of results, and none of which seem to offer the kind of foundation cream he was looking for. Admitting defeat, he returned to the coffee shop and joined his two companions.

"What's going on, Joe?" Sheila demanded.

Joe poured plenty of sugar into his white coffee, and took a mouthful. It tasted good, invigorating him. "It's something I've stumbled across this afternoon, and I need her ladyship's help to try and prove it." He pointed an irritable finger at Brenda who made an effort to focus on him.

"I don't think she's in any state to—"

Brenda interrupted with a slur. "I'm not as thunk as you drink I am."

"And you're not fooling anyone either," Joe told her.

Sheila intervened. "Tell me what it is, Joe."

He spent the next few minutes detailing his observations on Vivienne Foulkes, Peter Brandon, and particularly Diane Randleson, delivering his final conclusion which made Sheila's eyes opened wide.

"You're joking?"

"I wish I were. But remember, it's only a suspicion. I

could be way off the mark. But consider this. If I'm right, if Diane, Vivienne, and Brandon are organised and carrying out these thefts, what price Renata found out? Remember, Diane said she and Renata hardly knew each other. So let's imagine Renata found out, and threatened to blow it wide open. Now, we know that Diane didn't murder her, but can we say the same for Vivienne or Brandon?"

Sheila was silent for a few moments, tossing the question over and over in her mind, thinking, recalling the previous evening in the dining room. At length, she focused on Joe. "No. I can't swear that they were in the dining room at the time. Vivienne Foulkes was there after Margot made her announcement, but was she there before? I don't know. If you're right, Joe, it means that Vivienne probably dealt with Renata, while Peter Brandon broke into our chalet."

"That's exactly the way I see it. I don't know whether he fits the height profile Kirsty worked out from the video, but I'm going to confront him – and Vivienne – when I get back to Sun Kissed. In the meantime I need madam, there, to check out Diane, see if I'm right. There's only one way it can be done."

Sheila raised her eyebrows inviting further elucidation, and Joe went on to explain exactly what he wanted of Brenda, whereupon Sheila became irritated.

"That's awful."

"I know. But let's face it, do you want to do it? I certainly can't. If I'm wrong, I'll wind up doing time for assault."

"The same applies to Brenda."

A spark formed in Joe's imagination. "Not while she drunk, it doesn't. She could stumble or trip."

Sheila looked at that friend now in danger of nodding off to sleep over her coffee. "The state she's in, how are you going to get the message across?"

"I'll play it by ear. Our first problem is getting her back to Sun Kissed."

It was not an easy task. Brenda lolled and swayed between them as they helped her along the main shopping thoroughfare, and out to the car park, where they struggled further to get her into Sheila's Fiat. Eventually, with her settled, Joe pulled a seat belt around her, took the bags of shopping from Sheila and dropped them in the boot. Sheila climbed in behind the wheel of her car, Joe climbed into his, cursed the heat, and led the way from the car park out onto the main road, turning south for Gibraltar Point.

Twenty minutes later, they pulled into the parking area at the rear of their chalet, and repeated the struggle, getting Brenda into the kitchen and from there to the bedroom where they laid her down and let her drift off to sleep. They moved back to the living room and Sheila stationed herself as far from the windows as she could, and insisted he keep the blinds closed.

"Give her an hour. I'll leave you with her. For now, I'm off to see Foulkes and Brandon."

As he reached door, Sheila stayed him. "Just a minute. Aren't you flying off half-cocked over this? I mean, you have absolutely no evidence."

"I have Brandon's behaviour. I swear to you, Sheila, he ducked back in that chalet when he saw me knocking on Diane Randleson's door."

"And how will you approach them?"

He grinned at her. "With my usual, Sanford-bred level of tact and diplomacy."

"Wouldn't it be simpler to throw a petrol bomb through their window?"

"Yes, but considering the price of petrol, it would be a lot more expensive."

He stepped out of the front door, and concentrating his eye on the upper level and roofline of the chalets, made his way to reception where he rang the bell. When Margot appeared, he looked past her and towards a calendar bearing a picture of St Ives, Cornwall.

"Here again, Mr Murray. What is it this time?"

"I need more information from you."

"You could be considered quite a nuisance."

"I'm used to it. Where I come from everyone considers me a nuisance, but it doesn't put me off." A quick glance into the stern set of her eyes told him he was not winning her over. "Look, Margot, you hired me. You want me to pin down this thief. To do that I need your assistance. I'll get there, believe me, but not without some help from you."

She raised the counter. "Come through."

Håkan was working on his computer once again, and greeted Joe with a thin smile. "Good afternoon, Joe. Progress?"

Joe sat and this time fixed his eye on a portrait of a race horse and jockey visible over Håkan's right shoulder. He was not a betting man so he would never identify either the horse or its rider, but it was a useful focal point allowing him to avoid the spread of skin before him.

"Progress? Some, but I need to know what you know first."

Håkan must have noticed Joe's refusal to make eye contact. "Tell me something, do you have trouble looking me in the eye?"

"No. It's the rest of you I have problems with. At least until you put some clothes on."

"You've been here a day and half. I thought you would be used to it by now."

"If I'd been here a year and a half I don't think I'd be used to it. Now can we concentrate on more important matters? Like your thefts?"

"Ah. Of course. What is it you want to know?"

"Whatever you know about the three-way relationship between Diane Randleson, Vivienne Frankland, and Peter Brandon."

Håkan appeared blank. "I didn't know there was anything between them."

"They were together in Randleson's chalet earlier and when I went to speak to her, Brandon was coming out of a chalet further down the line. When he saw me, he ducked back in again. According to Randleson they were offering their condolences for Renata Chappell."

Maggot shrugged. "That sounds reasonable."

"And I'd be tempted to agree but last night Randleson told

us that Renata was a loose friend not a lover or a close buddy. Just a pal. And it doesn't explain why Brandon ducked out of sight when he saw me."

"What are you saying, Joe? That they're responsible for Renata's death?"

"It's possible, but that's a matter for the police. I'm interested in your serial thefts." He shuffled his seat closer to the desk. A mistake because it brought him a full frontal view of Margot which he could cheerfully have lived without.

He spent the next couple of minutes outlining his suspicions regarding the trio, the same suspicions he and Sheila had arrived at, and the Edströms listened to him before Håkan responded with something not quite outrage but not calm either.

"I find this very difficult to believe. We've known Vivienne Foulkes for a number of years and there has never been even a hint of suspicion about her."

"You know, I exposed a killer in Scarborough the Christmas before last. Civil servant just like Vivienne and Diane. Not a natural killer. Just snapped. Don't let appearances fool you. What about Brandon. Is he a member here?"

"First visit," Margot agreed. "He's a civil servant too. They'll never tell you what department they work for because—"

"Yes. I've had that debate with Diane already. You do seem to attract a lot of civil servants."

Maggot had a ready explanation. "Hardly surprising since I spent many years in the Civil Service before Håkan and I set up Sun Kissed. And before you press any further, Mr Murray, I won't tell you which department I worked in, but my naturist convictions were well-known amongst my colleagues and you wouldn't believe how far and fast word can spread in public service. That might have had some influence."

"Judging by the number of times I get into an argument at Sanford Town Hall followed by a visit from Environmental Health, I'd believe it."

Chapter Sixteen

When Joe knocked on the door of chalet #22, Peter Brandon opened it, glanced to Joe's left and right, as if expecting him to be accompanied, and then focussed on his visitor. "Yes?"

Joe looked over the man's shoulder. "We need to talk, you, me and Viv Foulkes. Put some clothes on and let me in."

"Why—"

Joe cut off the inevitable protest. "If you don't talk to me, I'll call the cops and tell them what I know about you two and Diane Randleson."

Brandon tutted. "Wait there."

The door closed and Joe was left standing there, wondering just how many of those sun worshippers lounging around the crystal blue of the swimming pool were looking at him, trying to work out what he was up to. When he scanned the crowd, he noticed many heads turning as if looking away from him, amongst them Pollitt, the Welsby/Simpson partnership, and further back, Kesteven and Ormond.

Let them look, was his attitude. It was the way of people. Wasn't he just the same, especially when working on a case? Hadn't it been that very inquisitiveness which made him spot Foulkes and Brandon joining Diane Randleson? What he had to say to the people in #22 was no concern of anyone's, other than, perhaps, the slight chance of recovering the stolen property from the burglary victims.

It seemed to him that door was taking its time opening, and he had a vision of Foulkes and Brandon hurrying out the back, jumping into a car and running off. He rapped the door again. No response.

He was getting ready to raise his voice, reiterate his threat to go to the police when Brandon yanked the door open and glowered. "How long do you think it takes us to dress at our age?"

Joe noticed that, unlike other members, the man had not merely put on a robe, but was fully dressed in business suit, the shirt collar open, tie hanging loose.

"You didn't have to go to that trouble."

"As it happens, I have to be in Skegness."

With your fence, no doubt. The thought rushed into Joe's head before he could stop it, but it made a kind of sense. What sort of appointment would anyone have at this hour on a Friday afternoon other than a meeting in a bar with someone ready to take the stolen goods off his hands?

When Brandon stepped back to let him in, he was not surprised to find Vivienne similarly attired, ready for an 'appointment'… with a glass or two if anyone wanted Joe's opinion.

"Going anywhere nice?" Joe asked.

"The Rep theatre, as a matter of fact. An amateur performance of Lear."

"Well, let's hope it doesn't have as many deaths as Hamlet did a couple of years back."

He expected them to be puzzled, to ask for clarification, at least query the number of deaths Shakespeare had put into each play, but they did not. It was almost as if they knew, and as a result their interest amounted to disinterest.

"So what is it you think we can do for you, Mr Murray?" Vivienne asked.

"Your relationship with Diane Randleson."

Brandon denied it. "We have no relationship with Ms Randleson."

"Yet I saw you call on her earlier."

Vivienne answered too quickly for Joe's liking. "We were returning a copy of the script for King Lear which she loaned us earlier in the week."

Joe scanned his memory. He had seen no sign of any paperback, hardback, or anything resembling a script on his visit to Diane. He decided that if he was going to throw them, now was as good a time as any.

"She says you called to offer your condolences for Ms Chappell."

Vivienne blushed. Brandon was made of sterner stuff. "Well naturally, we commiserated with her. It would be impolite to do anything else."

"You were commiserating for a little longer than I'd expect. And then you ducked out of the way when you saw me knocking on her door. I tell you, Mr Brandon, I have a different idea of what you were doing, one that links my investigation with the murder of Renata Chappell."

"What are you talking about, man?"

Forcing himself to remain calm, convinced that he had it right, Joe outlined his theory and watched their reactions which ranged from stunned to outright disbelief.

When he finally fell silent, Brandon plugged the gap. "Are you finished?"

"Aside from waiting for your comments, yes."

"Well, here's my comment. Get out. Before I throw you out."

Joe stood. Even with a man like Brandon he was never sure enough about himself to take on a physical confrontation. "You leave me with no choice. I've a report to put together, and then I'll be taking it to both Håkan and the cops. Thanks for your time."

Joe left nothing to chance. On the offchance that Brandon might follow him, when he stepped out into the searing heat of the late afternoon, he made his way hurriedly towards the bar, intending to circle the crowd at the top of the pool, to get to his chalet. A glance over his shoulder, revealed that he need not have rushed away. Neither Foulkes nor Brandon were behind him.

But Bill Welsby was in front of him, and as Joe made the top of the pool, Welsby left his sun lounger and blocked the way.

"Have you learned anything, Murray?"

"Yes. I've learned I'm sick and tired of this sodding place and the people in it. Now would you mind getting out of the way?"

"I want to know—"

Joe cut him off. "Back off, Welsby. I don't need you in the altogether to tell me where to kick."

As Welsby moved to one side, Joe passed him, hurried around the head of the pool, and down to the chalet where he found Sheila feeding strong black coffee to Brenda, who was not quite sober, but more aware of reality than when they first left her to sleep it off.

"How did you get on?" Sheila asked.

"They blanked me." Joe nodded at Brenda. "It's down to her now. Without her confirming my suspicions, I've got nothing, and I think both Foulkes and Brandon know that. Is Brenda gonna be all right?"

Sheila checked her watch. "I wouldn't go as far as all right, but she should be suitable for what you want doing. The biggest problem we might have is getting the idea across to her and getting her to keep quiet about it." A look of concern crossed her face. "Are you sure of your facts, Joe?"

"No. Why do you think I did Brenda to check it out?" He too checked the time. "Quarter past six. Time I was getting a shower and a shave and changing for dinner. I'll leave you with her."

To give credit, the bathrooms at Sun Kissed were well-appointed and the water hot enough for Joe to luxuriate in a something longer than a five minute shower. A dedicated wet shaver, he needed water at the hottest, bearable temperature for the job and once again Sun Kissed came up to scratch. When he rejoined the two women fifteen minutes later, clean-shaven, doused in low-cost aftershave, he felt refreshed, ready to tackle anything and anyone. It was always the way. With Sheila and Brenda or members the 3rd Age Club backing him, he would take on all comers. It was only when he as alone and violence threatened to materialise that he would employ discretion in favour of valour.

Brenda was still sobering up, but she was now clear-headed and lucid enough to listen and understand what he wanted of her, and right away, she objected. "I'm not doing it. Hell, Joe, what do you take me for?"

"If I answered that on the basis of this afternoon's behaviour, you really wouldn't want to hear it. Brenda, I have to confirm my suspicions one way or the other, and we can't ask outright… Well, we could, but I know what kind of answer we'd get. If you could make this accidental—"

"How can I make such a move accidental?" Brenda interrupted. "It's impossible."

"Well, think of something."

"No."

"Please."

"Sod off."

Joe gave up. "That's it, then. Our entire case is binned. Unless we can find some other way of proving it, and right now, I'm out of ideas."

His admission of defeat was something they had rarely come across. Most of the time, whether running the café, organising events and excursions for the 3rd Age Club, Joe was never anything less than positive, a level of certainty which few people seemed to possess. And he usually delivered on that confidence. Now he was beaten and admitting to it, and his deflation touched a nerve in Brenda.

"Do you mean that, Joe? Is it really that vital, or are you just trying to wind me up so I'll agree to give it a go?"

"I just said, didn't I? I can't think of any other way. Renata Chappell would have been able to tell us, but she's dead, and if I'm right, it was one of those three who wasted her."

"While another one of them broke into this place," Sheila said, waving her arms loosely at the chalet. "Allow me to make a suggestion, Brenda. There is a way, less blatant than Joe's idea, but it depends on how well you can act the drunk."

Brenda guzzled black coffee. "The way I feel, it won't need much acting skill. Go ahead. I'm listening."

***

The dining room was half full when they walked in at half past seven and took a table in one corner. When Joe looked around, he had to give his quarry a silent round of applause. Had Diane, Vivienne and Brandon been sat together, it would have been obvious that they were comparing notes on Joe's visits earlier. But they were at different tables, and while it was true that occasional glances from one or other came their way, Diane was sat with Kesteven and Gina Ormond, while Vivienne and Brandon shared a table with Pollitt, who appeared to be hogging the conversation.

From the moment they sat down, Joe insisted that Brenda should make a habit of visiting the toilet regularly while putting on her drunk act, and its success was inadvertently vouchsafed by Ellis Allyn, their waiter.

"Is your friend all right?" he asked as he arrived to take their order.

"Tanked up," Joe reported.

"Oh. Right. One over the odds at lunchtime?"

"One?" Sheila protested. "Two or three over the odds. Now Joe, what are we having?"

"Well, fish and chips was always on the Friday teatime menu in our house when I was growing up, so I'll have the haddock and chips."

"Make that three," Sheila insisted and caught Joe's look of query. "She'll be all right with it. Trust me. The fried food will help soak up the alcohol."

Sheila also ordered a glass of house white and bottle of still water for Brenda, while Joe settled for a glass of lager.

Throughout the first course, Joe kept an eye on Diane, and she did not move. Vivienne did a couple of times, and so did Brandon, but Diane stayed in her seat. They were deliberating their desert order when she finally moved, and Joe nudged Brenda.

"Go for it."

They watched her meander after Diane, Joe keeping an eye on Vivienne and Brandon, but neither appeared to be paying any attention.

The pair were gone for some time and Joe began to worry that Diane had rumbled the plan and was threatening Brenda. He was about to suggest that Sheila should check, when the two appeared at the door, Brenda smiling, reeling, and obviously making excuses for herself, Diane nodding in a manner which suggested impatience rather than annoyance. As if she wished this drunken woman would leave her alone.

Finally, they separated, and still weaving, Brenda returned to the table. Casting a glance around to ensure no one was taking any notice, she whispered, "It's definite."

"You're sure?" Joe asked.

"I might be half cut, Joe, but I still know the difference."

"That's good enough for me. Once we've had dinner, I'll bell Kirsty Hinch and get her down here. With a bit of luck, we should be able to present Håkan with his bill tomorrow, and we can have the rest of the weekend to ourselves."

Sheila's hopes rose with Joe's final words. "In Skegness? Not here?"

Joe chuckled. "I'm with you, Sheila, and I think Brenda might be as well. We can book into a hotel for the weekend, can't we?"

While they chewed their way through apple pie and custard, they talked about their plans for Saturday and Sunday, which inevitably meant more shopping for the women, and Joe's determination to pay a visit to The Tipsy Cow. At one point, Joe noticed Diane talking to Vivienne, but they noticed him and promptly parted company.

They were through with desert, when Kirsty Hinch and Nigel Brightwood walked into the dining room. They looked around, focused on the trio, and made their way through the tables.

Joe beamed a smile of welcome. "Talk of the devil. I was going to ring you, Kirsty, the minute I've finished my dinner."

Kirsty did not smile. "Joseph Murray, Sheila Riley, Brenda Jump, I'm arresting you on suspicion of public order offences. I must caution you…"

Chapter Seventeen

Under vehement protests which made them the centre of attention in the Sun Kissed dining room, they were bundled into the back of a van with two uniformed officers, and when Joe demanded answers of Kirsty, she excused herself.

"Nothing to do with me. It's Dudley Nichols. He's calling the shots."

They were driven to the police station in Skegness and kept in separate holding cells for about forty-five minutes until Nichols was ready for them, at which point they were led to an interview room which appeared more like a small briefing room. The table was large, circular, there were half a dozen chairs in place, and no sign of any recording equipment.

Nichols was alone when he came into the room and sat facing them, his face a mask of thunder. "Didn't I warn you? Keep your bloody nose out, I said, didn't I?"

If he believed he had the exclusive on moodiness, he was mistaken. Sheila was fuming, Brenda likewise, and when Nichols made his announcement, it was Joe, almost ready to explode, who came back at him.

"You never said anything of the kind. You asked what we knew about Carol Liddle's work, and you got our answers. You also got a guarantee that if we learned anything, we would bring it to you. As it turned out, we didn't learn anything. Well, nothing about what you and your people are interested in… whatever it is. But we did learn something about what's been going on at Sun Kissed the last three months, and it's ten to one that the three scroats we were looking at are the same ones who murdered that poor girl the other night. Now you tell us, why the hell were we dragged here under arrest?"

Nichols was not ready for backing down. "Just what is it you think you've learned about Diane Randleson, Vivienne Foulkes, and Peter Brandon?"

It was Brenda who replied. "I can tell you that Diane Randleson isn't a woman. Those beautiful boobs are falsies. I know. When we were in the ladies, I played drunk and fell against her, shoving my face right into her bazookas and I knew right away. She's all man." She pointed at Joe. "And it was Joe who rumbled it."

Joe picked up the argument. "She – correction, he is using theatrical make-up in burnt orange. Whether you know it or not, Nichols, it's almost impossible for a man to hide five o'clock shadow. When I checked up, drag queens use heavy make-up to cover it, and the best stuff is burnt orange. I found a jar of that same stuff in Randleson's chalet, and as I was coming out, he – or she – or it – ran a hand over his cheek to make sure that the stubble wasn't showing through. Diane Randleson is a man."

"I know."

"Right. So what is she doing…" Joe's furious tirade came to an abrupt halt. "What did you say?"

"I said, I know." Nichols picked up the internal extension, hit a couple of digits, and then spoke softly into it. He put the phone down and glowered at Joe. "Do you know what a pain in the butt you are? All three of you?"

"You weren't saying that a couple of years ago when we cracked the Hamlet murders for you, were you?"

"Not to your face, but I was behind your back. I knew you'd be a problem when I learned that the Edströms had called you in. Well, in a minute, you're gonna learn everything, and then you're gonna do like I say and keep your mouths shut."

"You don't have an army big enough to shut us up," Joe challenged and Sheila shushed him.

The door opened, and Kirsty stepped in. She was not alone. To the surprise of all three, she was accompanied by Diane Randleson, now dressed as a man, wearing a smart business suit in dark grey, with a white shirt and dark tie. He was followed by Vivienne Foulkes, and Peter Brandon. They ranged themselves alongside Nichols, on the opposite side of the table to Joe and his friends, and Kirsty on the other side of her immediate boss.

"I took the liberty of ordering tea, Chief Inspector," Vivienne said. "For our guests as well as ourselves."

"Very good, ma'am."

Joe was speechless, Brenda, too, but Sheila soon found her voice, and she addressed Nichols. "Guests, Mrs Foulkes? Not from the way we've been treated." She honed an icy stare on Nichols. "You may or may not remember, Chief Inspector, but my husband was a long serving police officer. I'm no lawyer, but I do know a little about the law, and as far as I'm concerned, you have arrested us on a false pretext, which is presumably something to do with these three people."

"Mr Nichols did as he was ordered, Mrs Riley." Again it was Vivienne who spoke. "You're not under arrest and you never were. It was an expedient, a means of getting you out of Sun Kissed to the police station where we could speak to you in detail, and impress upon you the need for complete secrecy." She switched her attention to Joe. "When we spoke to him, a very good friend of yours, Superintendent Terence Cummins, the local station commander in Sanford, told us that you were one of the best, Mr Murray. He also said that you had a habit of getting to the right answers for all the wrong reasons. In this case, you arrived at the wrong answer for all right reasons. Allow me to introduce myself and my two colleagues properly. I am Detective Chief Superintendent Vivienne Foulkes of the Lincolnshire Constabulary. This is Detective Superintendent Peter Brandon of the Lincolnshire Constabulary, and the gentleman you know as Diane Randleson, is Detective Constable Daniel Anderson, of Lincoln CID, temporarily seconded to our unit."

Joe was certain that his jaw fell. "You're cops?" So much became clear to Joe. "So that's why you didn't need me to explain about the Hamlet murders. You already knew." He pointed a finger of accusation at Nichols. "And he told you about Terry Cummins. No wonder the street scroats call you filth."

"Not a term we're happy with, Murray," Brandon commented, "but yes, we're police officers. Vivienne and I are part of the same serious crimes squad as Chief Inspector Nichols. DC Anderson is a volunteer, and the focus of our operation, is… Pardon me, was, Renata Chappell."

"Until she was murdered," Anderson said. "Frankly, Mr Murray, I'm glad you and your friends were in the dining room that night, because I would have been the obvious suspect and that would have blown my cover wide open. Thanks to you, I was able to maintain my undercover role." He gave Brenda a pointed stare. "As for you, Mrs Jump, that wasn't very bright falling against me like that. I guessed Murray was already suspicious after he picked up the jar of theatrical make-up. Your behaviour in the ladies, confirmed it. I had no choice but to call my bosses."

Brenda refused to be fazed. "It wasn't all an act, you know. I was a bit tiddly. I had about half a bottle of Campari in The Tipsy Cow at lunchtime, and I hadn't entirely sobered up. But if you want to blame anyone, blame Joe. It was his idea." She laughed. "Mind, he told me to check your landing gear a bit lower down."

The young detective blanched, and Joe took the lead.

"Don't be laying it on us, Anderson. I was watching all three of you this afternoon, and as undercover cops go, all three of you might as well be carrying placards saying, 'I'm behaving suspiciously'." He posed his next question to Vivienne. "Well, now that we know who you are, don't you think it's time you brought us up to speed? What has Renata Chappell done to interest you people?"

"Blackmail, Mr Murray," Vivienne said. "She doesn't work alone, but over the last few years, she and her friends – whoever they are – have hit on some seriously high-ranking, powerful targets and taken a fortune from them. No matter how hard we tried, we could not get any of the victims to testify. The case was passed to me and with Peter's help, we came up with the scheme you stumbled upon."

Anderson took up the story. "The boss—" he nodded at Vivienne "— asked me if I'd mind posing as a crossdresser, a civil servant with the ear of several, senior politicians."

The admission rang an instant bell with Joe. "Liddle's story."

"Correct," Brandon agreed. "We don't know where Ms Liddle got the tipoff, but we suspect it might have been Chappell herself. And by the way, her name wasn't Renata Chappell."

Sheila was next to comment. "The only thing is, Liddle insisted that she was pursuing a Right Honourable someone or other. To my knowledge, civil servants, no matter how high they might be, are never granted such a title."

"Liddle putting one over on you, Mrs Riley," Vivienne suggested. "We don't know for sure because she refused to divulge any information, and, naturally, she didn't know who we were. Chief Inspector Nichols dealt with her, pretended to be a member of the Intelligence services and threatened her with the Official Secrets Act." She smiled. "She's not the only one who can play silly, secret games."

It was left to Joe to drag the discussion back on track. "You were saying Chappell's name wasn't really Chappell."

Brandon nodded. "Correct. She was Rhoslyn Clausen, born Dusseldorf in the late nineteen seventies. She's wanted in Germany on charges of extortion, too. She came to this country sometime during the late noughties."

Joe pressed again. "And how many people does she work with? One, two, a mob?"

"We're not sure. We think no more than one or two, but her associates are much more secretive than she ever was."

Vivienne picked up the tale. "Even so, she proved to be a resourceful young woman. It took us a long time to latch onto her. She could change her appearance almost at will, and we had a devil of a time pinning her down, and as I've already hinted, we still haven't identified her partners. When our colleagues in London finally pulled her in, they couldn't get enough evidence to make it stick, and when they consulted the German authorities, they didn't have enough solid evidence, either. She was running rings round us, and that's when we came up with our sting." She gestured with an open hand at Anderson. "It wasn't as difficult to set up as you might imagine. I really am a naturist. My colleagues are aware of it, and I suffered the usual ribbing when I was younger. Less so now that I'm of a senior rank. All we needed was a volunteer to play the part of Diane Randleson, and lead Chappell along. Daniel was doing a fine job, and Renata had begun to turn the screws on him, insisting that it had to be worth a lot of money to keep quiet about Daniel-Diane's, er, idiosyncrasies. We calculated we needed another week, two at the most and we would have her, and once she was hooked, we were sure she would betray her partners."

Joe understood at once. "Except that someone bumped her off before you could nail her. It explains why none of you ran for it after she was murdered. Aside from the way it would point the finger of suspicion at you, you want to nick the killer, don't you?"

Vivienne shook her head. "Nothing of the kind. That's a job for Inspector Hinch and her crew. No, Mr Murray. As I keep saying, the one thing we're sure of is that Renata, Rhoslyn, call her what you will, does not work alone. She never has, but her contacts have never been identified. We believe they are at Sun Kissed now." She checked her watch. "And they'll be on their way home in a few hours if we don't do something."

The narrative switched to Brandon. "With all due respect to Superintendent Foulkes's opinion, I'm pretty sure she was killed by her partners."

"Why?" Joe asked. "I mean why would they do it, not why do you suspect them?"

"We don't know." Brandon shrugged. "There's an old saying about thieves falling out, isn't there? And if I'm right, then any arrest will fall within our remit, not Inspector Hinch's."

Alongside Nichols, Kirsty appeared stone-faced, but Joe could see the anger in her eyes. "And how do you feel about that, Kirsty?"

"I'm a professional police officer, Joe, so I'll leave you to work out how I feel."

Joe nodded in sympathy. "I'd feel the same way if someone opened a café right next door to mine." He faced Vivienne again. "So what is it you want from us?"

"Your silence primarily."

"Bit difficult. Y'see we're at Sun Kissed for a reason. Håkan Edström wants to know who's been nicking from the guests."

"And if we offered to pay your bill and let you go home without er, cracking the case, as it were?"

"I'd tell you where to shove it." Joe lounged in his seat. He was still seething with anger, but put out a fake air of nonchalance. He knew it would not fool his friends, and it was questionable whether it would trick the police, but even if it did not, it would give them a kick where he felt they most deserved it. "I have my reputation to think of, you see. Do I really want to be known as a detective who can't do the job?"

Brenda chuckled. "He does have a point, you know. His reputation is bad enough as it is."

Brandon came on a little harder. "And if we threaten you with arrest?"

This time it was Sheila who challenged them. "On what charge? As far as we're concerned, we've done nothing wrong, and if you try to trump up charges, you'll find we're more than capable of meeting you head on."

"We can even call on a scumbag reporter to back us up," Joe said. "And you wouldn't believe how good we are at drumming up publicity. Drop the threats, Brandon, and as for you, Mrs Foulkes, you know what you can do with your payoff." He sat upright, and leaned on the table. "Here's the deal, and it's not subject to negotiation. We will keep our mouths shut about you and your silly game of charades, and if we should turn up anything, even the slightest hint as to who might have been working with Renata Chappell, we'll ring your bell."

Vivienne Foulkes smiled. "That was precisely what we expected of you, and we're happy enough with that arrangement. Inspector Hinch will arrange transport back to Sun Kissed for you."

Chapter Eighteen

With the time coming up to ten o'clock, Sheila and Brenda climbed into the rear seats of Kirsty's saloon, while Joe took the front passenger seat, and from the moment she drove out of the car park, Kirsty was full of apology.

"I'm sorry, ladies, Joe. It was nothing to do with me."

"And we don't blame you," Sheila said. "Do we, Joe?"

He answered with a noncommittal grunt. Not that he blamed Kirsty, but his mind was on other things, too occupied to deliver a proper reply.

The car cruised along North Parade, heading towards Skegness centre, and the lights from bars, clubs, amusement arcades, and the fairground lit the sky, the multi-coloured beacons casting a balm of joy into the air, a message of freedom, of delights, even hedonism, and it reminded him of Blackpool, the main difference being that the Golden Mile of Lancashire's Premier resort, was actually two miles from the foot of the tower to the entrance of the Pleasure Beach, whereas here in Skegness, it was slightly less than half a mile from the point where they joined the promenade to the famed clock tower, where Kirsty turned right into the town centre, to pick up the southbound road for Gibraltar Point and Sun Kissed Holiday Park.

The mental comparison with Blackpool took him back to the Sanford 3rd Age Club's two outings, one just before the New Year, the other from a couple of years previously. Both times he had been dragged into murder mysteries, both times he had succeeded, but at some cost. Over the previous Twixmas two good friends had been killed, and on the 3rd Age Club's previous visit, he had come home after Easter to find The Lazy Luncheonette burned to the ground. Not long after that, the man who had sponsored that act of arson was found murdered, and Joe spent four days in HM Prison Sanford under suspicion of having killed him.

Everything turned out for the better, but he had never forgotten that terrible time. And here he was again, released from the police station having spent the better part of three hours in custody. It called into question his motive. The murder of Renata Chappell was nothing to do with him or his friends, the questionable antics of the serious crime people in the shape of Vivienne Foulkes, Peter Brandon, and Daniel Anderson were no concern of his, and yet, like the time he had been suspected of murder, he and his friends were dragged into it without so much as a by your leave.

In Cleethorpes the previous year, Sheila had recommended that he put his private investigations on a professional footing by undergoing the necessary training, and acquiring the licence. It seemed like a good idea. In practice, he was beginning to doubt it. Work was scarce, and if he had no licence, there was a good chance that Håkan Edström would never have called him, and he wouldn't have ended up spending three hours locked in a cell and engaged in a head-to-head with seriously senior police officers.

To add to the angst, they had made absolutely no progress. His three suspects turned out to be anything but thieves, they had managed to let Edström's files fall into criminal hands, he had lost an expensive laptop computer, and between them, he and his friends had absolutely nothing to show for it.

"Well?"

Kirsty's voice brought him back to the reality of her car, now cruising out of Skegness towards their destination.

"Sorry. I wasn't listening. What did you say?"

"Are you any further forward on the thefts?"

"Aside from accusing your bosses, no."

"And you've no idea who might have cut Renata Chappell's throat?"

"Again, no."

Kirsty chuckled. "Not up to your usual mark, Joe."

From the back seat, Brenda piped up. "He's distracted,

Kirsty. He and I spent the night together, but he was too tired to be of any use to me."

Sheila tutted, Kirsty laughed aloud and Joe muttered something unprintable under his breath.

As they passed out of the town, he asked, "Did you run checks on those people I asked about, Kirsty?"

"Yes, and all came up clean and green. Sorry, Joe."

He groaned. "The staff too?"

"Yep. I'm afraid so. I told you Ellis Allyn had form, but like I said, it was mainly for drunkenness, fighting, run-of-the-mill stuff for a seaside town. He's never been a tealeaf."

Joe half turned in his seat to look at his friends. "What say we call it a draw tomorrow morning? Tell Håkan we don't know anything, cut our losses, and clear off home?"

"You mean hang around Skegness for another couple of days, Joe," Sheila said. "Brenda and I are in no rush to get back to Sanford."

"Yeah, well, you know what I mean."

Brenda shook her head and tutted at the same time. "Håkan won't like that, Joe. You lost his files, and that could get him into a lot of trouble, which means he's unlikely to pay your bill. He might even sue you for losing them."

"You have a better idea, do you, Brenda?"

She fell silent, and Joe took it as a sign that he had (for once) won the argument.

"I'll have a word with him when we get back." He concentrated on Kirsty. "I'm sorry, girl. This one really has us beat."

"Don't worry about it, Joe. It's not your fault if the Edströms go bust, is it?"

The remark puzzled Joe. "Go bust? They're not that near the line, surely?"

The entrance to Sun Kissed appeared ahead, and Kirsty turned in. "Maybe, maybe not. All I know is that when Edström came to see me on Monday, he was complaining that the thefts were costing him a lot of money. Not the thefts, per se, but members dropping out." Parking the car, shutting down the engine, she waved at the buildings around them. "I don't know how much it costs to keep a site like this going, but it must be a pretty penny, and if their income's down, it's likely to be eating into their profits, and with the general state of the economy, you have to wonder how much longer they can go on." Kirsty brightened up a little. "There you go, people. Back at your little holiday camp. Let me know if and when you're leaving, and in the meantime, if you turn anything up, give me a bell."

They climbed out of the car, watched her leave, and Sheila aimed the remote at her Fiat. "I'm not coming in there. I'll get straight back to my digs. Can we meet for breakfast at the same place tomorrow morning?"

Both Joe and Brenda were too tired to argue with her. "Edie's Eatery," Brenda said. "We'll be there about half past nine."

They stood by and watched her leave, then turned into the building. "You having a word with his lordship, Joe?" Brenda asked.

"I'd better do, yes."

"You're telling him we're chucking the towel in?"

"No. Not yet. I need to think about what Kirsty's just told us."

Brenda frowned. "I don't know what you mean."

Joe tapped the side of his nose, made his way to the counter, and rang the bell. "Trust me, Brenda. I know what I'm doing."

Margot appeared from the rear office. "Oh. They've released you?"

"It was a lot of nonsense, Mrs Edström," Brenda explained. "We'd done nothing wrong, but certain of your members didn't see it the same way."

Joe nudged her to be quiet. "I just called to let you know we were back, Margot, and we'll be back on the case first thing in the morning." He smiled at Brenda. "Fancy a nightcap?"

She smiled back. "I fancy a lot more than that, Joe."

"Dream on."

***

It was coming up to midnight when they finally got back to the chalet. A couple of lagers, and another two Camparis saw Brenda slipping once more into a semi-drunken haze, and after a cup of tea, most of which she spilled, she went to bed, while Joe sat at the small table, making notes by hand.

It was annoying watching the pens scribble its way across the page; annoying and slow. His handwriting, for which he had won certificates at school, was now not much better than a barely legible scrawl, and he had to wonder how his crew at The Lazy Luncheonette managed to interpret it. He also had to wonder how he, himself would interpret it in the clear light of day after a night's sleep which would rob him of the ideas he was supposed to follow.

Even so, he persevered, plodding along, formulating his case, pulling together the tiny hints which led to what he considered an inescapable conclusion. True, there were those areas which were difficult to explain, but Joe had been at the game long enough to press for a full explanation, even if some of those miscreants ended up pleading 'not guilty' when the case came to court.

By the time he had finished, however, he was content with his deductions, more so because not only had he identified the thief of Sun Kissed, but also Renata Chappell's killer. That would almost certainly put Vivienne Foulkes, Peter Brandon, and Dudley Nichols's noses out of joint. With the clock reading a little after twelve-thirty, he killed the lights, and made his way to bed.

***

Saturday dawned with another, cloudless sky, promising searing temperatures. Joe was out of bed for half past seven, enjoyed a cup of tea in the chalet, with the front blinds open about twelve inches, watching the pool attendant, a young man clad only in a pair of swimming shorts, sorting, tidying the sun loungers for the day ahead.

Closer to the reception block, he could see Håkan Edström fussing with a broom. Joe understood. One of the simplest ways of keeping costs down was to take on the menial tasks such as sweeping, mopping floors. At The Lazy Luncheonette, it was part and parcel of the crew's work, and he was not exempt.

He was pleased to see Håkan, although he doubted that the proprietor would be glad to see him. At half past seven, he made a quick phone call to Sheila (he knew she would be up and about) told her of his plans, and asked her to run a brief check to see what information she could deliver. With the time coming up to eight o'clock, she rang back and confirmed his ideas.

Armed with all the information he believed he would need, he woke Brenda, told her where he would be, and then stepped out of the front door, and made his way to reception where he rang the bell.

"Good morning, Mr Murray," Håkan greeted him. "It looks like another beautiful day ahead. Do you have information for us?"

"No. Not really. But we do need to talk. And I'd prefer if you and your wife were present, both of you dressed."

His tone of voice, the set of his face, transmitted his mood.

"This sounds serious," Håkan commented.

"It is. I'll wait here until you're both ready."

While he waited he looked around the notices of local attractions. He was certain he could remember a railways advertisement from when he was a child in which Skegness featured strongly, and, of course, it was where Butlins established the first camp sometime back in the pre-war years. He wondered just how people back then would react to a site like Sun Kissed.

When Håkan returned, wearing his familiar, thin bathrobe, he raised the end of the counter, and escorted Joe through to the inner office, where Margot, similarly clad, waited for them.

"So, what is it we can do for you, Joe?" Håkan asked.

"It's simple enough. I want to know why you bothered hiring me when you and your wife are the resident thieves, and how you hoped you'd get away with murdering Renata Chappell."

Chapter Nineteen

The reaction of both husband and wife was nothing short of astonishment, but Joe had been playing the game long enough not to be fooled. Most criminals, whether by accident or design, were experts at masking their guilt, putting on an act. Some were more convincing than others, and he would include the Edströms in that number. If he were not so experienced, he might be prepared to accept their amazement as a genuine reaction.

It did not surprise him when Margot recovered first. As far as he was concerned she was guiltier than her husband. "Have you taken leave of your senses, Mr Murray?"

"No. In fact, I only came to them late last night when Inspector Hinch brought us back."

Håkan was sufficiently recovered. "I think you had better leave, Mr Murray, before—"

Joe interrupted. "I'm going nowhere. You see, there are three elements to every crime: means, motive, opportunity. We can't debate means. We know how Renata Chappell was murdered. So it came down to opportunity and motive. Sheila, Brenda, and I were in the dining room when that poor girl was killed, which means we could eliminate quite a number of people, including Dan…" Joe caught himself before he could deliver Daniel Anderson's real name, "… Diane Randleson and Carol Liddle amongst them. There were others we couldn't eliminate. Welsby and Simpson, Kesteven and Ormond, Trevor Pollitt. True, Pollitt would have been taking a hell of a chance sneaking into the ladies to kill that woman, but given that most of your members hang around in the nude all day, I'm sure he would have an excuse ready. But there were two people I never thought about. You two. Neither of you were anywhere to be seen until you, Margot, came into the dining room screaming that you found her dead."

"But I did," she protested. "And I find your suggestion that I could take the life of another human being not merely offensive, but obscene."

Joe ignored her bluster. "The other aspect we need to consider is motive, but the police gave me that yesterday. Renata Chappell wasn't Renata Chappell. I can't remember her real name, but she was German, and a professional blackmailer. A blackmailer in a place like this would have plenty of targets, but I wonder what kind of pressure she could have applied to you? Then Kirsty Hinch let it slip last night. You're on the verge of bankruptcy, aren't you?"

"Nonsense," Håkan snorted. "Times are hard, certainly. You're a businessman, you know how difficult the current economic climate is. We lost a few members, bookings are down, but that's only to be expected. We are not, however, on the point of folding, and I don't know where Inspector Hinch got such an idea."

"Apparently, you hinted at it when you spoke to her last Monday."

"Then she misunderstood what I was saying. These thefts are costing us a lot of money in terms of further reductions in bookings. And now you stand there, and have the audacity to suggest that we are actually carrying out the thefts. If that is the case, why then did we call you in?"

Joe put on a convincing mask of perplexity. "I think the word is verisimilitude. You're trying to lend credence to your efforts to track down the thieves, knowing full well that we wouldn't get anywhere."

Now Håkan laughed. "And for that I'm willing to pay over two thousand pounds? I think you're living in a dream world, Mr Murray, and if this is the sum total of your investigative abilities, then I think you should stick to running your café."

Joe waved the objection away. "Yeah, yeah. Heard it all before. Listen to me, both of you. You're in an awful lot of trouble, and the best thing you can do is cough up to the truth. I know what happened. Renata found out you were nicking from your members, she turned the screws, and you, Margot, dealt with her. I'll tell you something else, too. I had Mrs Riley run a check on you, Håkan, and you're a bit of a mystery. I always wondered what it was that would make a man like you leave his homeland for this country. You were a military man, weren't you? What were you? Some kind of saboteur? Your military career is shrouded in mystery." He turned his attention to Margot. "And what about you? You were a civil servant. What department was that? Ministry of Defence? Or maybe it was part of the Intelligence Services."

Håkan stood. "I think I've heard enough. I would prefer it if you and your colleagues were to pack your bags and leave, Mr Murray. If you are not off the site by 10 o'clock, I shall call the police and have you removed."

Joe chuckled. "You don't have to do that. I'll call the cops for you. I'm sure Kirsty Hinch will be only too glad to hear what I have to say."

"You really think she'll take on board this nonsense?" Margot asked. "For your information, Mr Murray, I worked for DEFRA, the Department for Environment, Food and Rural Affairs, not MI5."

Håkan backed his wife up. "And for your information, I was in the Swedish Armed Forces. That is because I was called up. National Service was still in force at the time. It was eventually abandoned in 2010, and then reinstated in 2017. There's nothing particularly mysterious about my time in the Swedish army. And as I told you when you first came to Sun Kissed, I came to this country because I met and fell in love with Margot, a woman who shared my enthusiasm for a naturist way of life."

Joe felt his irritation rising, but before he could protest, Håkan went on.

"And now, I would like you to leave. Don't bother to send a bill. It will not be paid. But after losing confidential files on both my members and my staff, you can expect to hear from my solicitor."

Joe got to his feet. "Have it your own way. I'll be back in a while with Kirsty Hinch."

He marched out of the office, and as he crossed the pool area, he took out his phone, switched off flight mode, and rang Kirsty.

"Joe. Where the hell have you been? I've been trying to get you for the last half-hour."

"Yeah, well, I got into a head-to-head with Edström, didn't I? Anyway, I've cracked your case for you. I know who murdered Renata."

"Yes. So do we. I have people on their way to Sun Kissed right now, but I need you here, Joe."

"Where? The police station?"

"As soon as you can. I need you to identify your laptop."

A sense of elation ran through him. "You've found it."

"Amongst a lot of other things, yeah."

He smiled into the phone. "I'll be there in twenty minutes, but I have to pack first. Edström's ordered us to leave."

"As soon as you can, Joe. Ignore Edström."

Kirsty terminated the call, Joe walked back into the chalet, where Brenda was in the process of swallowing a couple of paracetamol with her morning tea.

"Death warmed up," she said. "Did you sort it all?"

"I did. They're denying everything, and Håkan has told us to pack up and get out. On the other hand, Kirsty's insisted I get to the cop shop ASAP." He gave Brenda a lopsided grin. "Now you know me. I won't argue with the police."

She laughed. "Unless they're nicking you for dumping chip fat in the back lane. Hadn't we better ring Sheila?"

"I'll leave you to do it. I'd better get off to Skeggy."

Even though his car was at the rear, he left via the front. The pool area was sparsely populated, and it took a moment for him to recall that it was Saturday, changeover day. Many of the guest, members, whatever Edström chose to call them, would be ensconced in their chalets, packing, preparing for the journey home. He and his friends would not be far behind them, except that they would spend another night here in Skegness, enjoying themselves, revelling in the success of another case closed.

As he passed through reception, Håkan was at the counter. "I thought I asked you to leave, Mr Murray."

Joe's lip curled. "You did, but I've just had a call from the police station. They've found my laptop, hopefully covered in your DNA." Having made his point, he turned and went back the way he came. His sole purpose in going to reception was to wind Håkan Edström up a little further before the police arrived, and he explained as much to Brenda when he walked through the chalet to his car at the rear. Leaving her muttering on his childish, confrontational action, he climbed into his car, started the engine, let the windows down and pulled out of the parking slot to plod round to the main exit.

As he arrived so three police cars came hurrying in, and Sergeant Brightwood climbed out of the lead vehicle.

"They're in reception, son," Joe told him.

"Who?"

"The Edströms."

The sergeant scowled. "We're not here for the Edströms. And you'd better get moving. Inspector Hinch is waiting for you." Before Joe could take him to task, Brightwood marshalled his small team of uniformed officers, and they hurried into the reception building.

Joe was tempted to wait, but Brightwood's reminder that Kirsty was waiting for him, changed his mind. He pulled out of the park, turned left and accelerated along the narrow lane towards Skegness.

How was it possible that they were not arresting the Edströms? They were the guilty party... Well, guilty of Renata Chappell's murder.

Or were they?

As the car made its way along the main road into Skegness, juggling through the increasing vehicular and pedestrian traffic of the town centre, skimmed by the fairground and pier, Joe ran his deductions through his agile mind and came to the conclusion that he was right. They had murdered Renata Chappell. But that did not mean they were responsible for the thefts, and (of course) his laptop had turned up. Kirsty, he decided, had been right all along. The break-in was not connected to Renata's murder. It was not entirely coincidental that the burglary happened shortly after the killing. The thief had taken advantage of the distress and focus on the shocking events in the ladies toilets.

Score the police several brownie points for unmasking the thief or thieves, but Joe was the champion (as always). He had identified that poor girl's killers. Whether he would be paid for his efforts remained to be seen, but at least he would see justice done. Håkan and Margot Edström would go to prison, possibly for the rest of their lives, and he could take some satisfaction from that. A young constable – they all looked young at Joe's age – signed him in and escorted him to Kirsty's office, where his laptop sat on the desk. Even without lifting the lid, he recognised it.

"It is your initials scratched on the underside," Kirsty told him, "but we can't get into it. It's password protected."

"Of course it is. All my basic accounts are on there."

He pulled up a chair, sat down, raised the laptop lid, and the screen came to life. He typed in his 12-digit password, a combination of letters taken from the names of people closest to him, Sheila, Brenda, Lee, his niece, Gemma, followed by four numbers. When he hit the 'enter' key, the screen came to life with a view of The Lazy Luncheonette as seen from Doncaster Road. He tapped occasional keys, opening this program, that piece of software, folders of personal photographs, and at length, he nodded to Kirsty. "That's it. It's mine. Do you need to keep it for evidence?"

"Not especially. We found plenty of other stuff in her place."

"Her place?" Joe's voice spelled out its surprise. "Who is her?"

"Olga Dellon."

"The barmaid?"

Kirsty nodded. "I told you we knew about Ellis Allyn, but we have nothing on her. If you were looking at Ellis, Joe, you were looking at the wrong angle. She's the tealeaf. She came in first thing this morning, and handed over your laptop and a lot of other stuff, including Håkan Edström's missing files."

Joe was dumbfounded. "But the geezer we saw on my mini camera was a man."

"Yes. But Olga didn't take your laptop from your chalet. She took it from the people who stole it from you."

Joe looked upon the admission. "The Edströms. I bloody knew it."

Now it was Kirsty's turn to frown. "Margot and Håkan? What does it have to do with them?"

He delivered an exasperated sigh. "They're the ones who murdered Renata Chappell."

"I don't know where you got that idea from, Joe, but they had nothing to do with any of this. Right now, Nigel Brightwood should have the real perpetrators in cuffs."

Joe swam in a sea of confusion. "Well, who the hell are they?"

"Bill Welsby and Arabella Simpson."

Chapter Twenty

"What?" Joe's eyes popped and he was unable to string together any comments longer than the single word.

Faced with such obvious confabulation, Kirsty picked up the telephone, rang the canteen and ordered tea for both of them. She put down the phone, picked up her pen and toyed with it. "Maybe I'd better tell you exactly what happened."

Joe agreed. "It might be a good idea. I've just accused the Edströms of murder and theft."

She chuckled. "Oh dear. Is that why they asked you to leave?"

"What do you think?" Joe shut down the laptop. "What's been going on? Or aren't you allowed to tell me?"

"I don't have a problem telling you. Unlike Dudley, I trust you to keep it to yourself... or at least between you and your lady friends." Kirsty paused, obviously thinking about where to start. "As I said, it was Ellis and Olga carrying out the thieving. She came to us this morning terrified. Ellis is in hospital. He's been stabbed." She paused to let the news sink in. "Welsby and Simpson paid them a visit in the early hours of this morning. Don't ask me how they knew it was Ellis and Olga. They just did. There was a fight. Arabella stabbed Ellis and Olga ran for it. Problem was, Joe, none of the loot was stored at Ellis's place; Olga had it all. She ran from Ellis's flat, got to the beach, rang us, and then hid in the dunes, not far from the seal sanctuary. She was certain she heard Welsby and Simpson nearby, looking for her but they didn't find her, and of course, they didn't know where she lived. In any event, she made her way along the beach back to her place, where our people met her, and she let them in. I've seen the photographs, Joe. The place was like Aladdin's cave. She and Ellis planned to carry on taking what they could until the end of the season, about another eight weeks, then offloaded it for every penny they could get, and then leg it to Europe."

There was a knock on the door and a uniformed officer entered, ordered tea with them, and then disappeared.

Kirsty picked up her story. "We took a full statement from her, and we've been cataloguing the goods ever since. I recognised the laptop right away, and something else."

Taking a large swallow from her beaker, Kirsty reached down and ferreted through a stack of evidence bags spread around the floor close to her desk until she found what she was looking for.

Inside was a German passport, but it did not look like a modern, EU passport. Instead it was black, with the emblem of the old East Germany in the days before the Berlin Wall fell, emblazoned on the front, beneath which was the word, *Reispasse*, and along the bottom *Deutsche Demokratische Republik*.

"East Germany?" Joe wondered how many more surprises he could stand without spilling his tea.

"I'm not going to open it," Kirsty said. "I could be accused of tampering with evidence. But it's made for Annaliese Schlegel, a citizen of Berlin and – get this – a Stasi officer."

"Their cops," Joe commented.

"The picture matches Arabella Simpson." Kirsty dropped the evidence bag back in the box. "During the communist era, there were rumours – never confirmed – of death squads in the Stasi, and I'm not saying that Annaliese was a member of such a crew, but we're running checks with the German Embassy. When the wall came down, a lot of those Stasi people went on the run and they're still wanted. We're guessing that that's the case with Annaliese. We'll know more when we get hold of her and when the Germans come back to us."

Joe gulped down some tea. "So where does Renata Chappell fit into this?"

"Again, we're not sure, but remember, she was German too.

Both on the run, we think they met up in Germany, then made their way to this country on forged passports, and somewhere along the line, they bumped into Bill Welsby. Maybe they tried to screw him for big money. I don't know. If so, they bit off more than they could chew, and they formed a threesome. We still don't know enough about Welsby to be sure."

"And they fell out over something this week?"

"Almost certainly. Maybe Renata decided it was time to cut and run, go solo. After all, she was at the sharp end, wasn't she? She was the one digging the dirt, she was the one the British and German authorities were chasing. Maybe she asked for a bigger cut. Like I said, we don't know, but Annaliese took the opportunity to cut her in the ladies toilet at Sun Kissed. We'll know for certain later today. Forensic didn't get much from the crime scene, but if we find one trace of Annaliese Schlegel, it'll be enough. We'll have her bang to rights, and I guarantee that she'll take Welsby down with her." A broad grin spread across her pretty features. "And do you know how much pleasure it will give me to stuff it in Dudley Nichols face? Not to mention Vivienne Foulkes, Peter Brandon and Daniel Anderson."

"I can guess." Joe allowed his mind to drift over the things he had learned. "How's Ellis?"

"Bad, but the hospital reckon he'll survive. He'll be in dry dock for a week or three, and when he's discharged he still has charges to face. So does Dellon. Chances are we'll go easy on them because of the assistance they've given us in cornering the Welsby, Simpson, Chappell triangle. And naturally it's a feather in my cap. My first major case as top dog in CID, and I cracked it. Had a bit of luck, true, but I still got there."

Joe grunted. "I'm pleased for you. You deserve it."

Kirsty chuckled again. "Pleased? You could have fooled me, Joe. From the look on your face, you look anything but pleased."

"Yes, well, one of us has to face Håkan and Margot Edström… and apologise."

"Humble pie, my friend. Put your best dentures in and get chewing."

***

Joe was not a man to grovel, but he owed the Edströms an apology. When he faced them, neither of them bothered to dress, and Joe was left offering profuse apologies to St Ives as depicted on the calendar behind the reception counter. His reluctance to make eye contact lent no sincerity to his apology and when he was through explaining what had transpired, Håkan left him in no doubt as to his mood or the situation vis-à-vis Joe's bill.

"You have enjoyed free accommodation, yet at the same time you have criticised our way of life, upset a number of our members, amongst them a senior police officer and two of her colleagues, and notwithstanding your audacity in accusing my wife and I of theft and murder, you did nothing to clear up the problem I asked you to handle. Indeed, it was the police who cleared up those thefts. I fail to see why I should pay you one penny. In fact, I should be charging you for the cost of accommodation."

Joe bristled. "Try it. See how far it gets you."

"I will not waste any more time with you, Mr Murray. I want you and your colleagues off my site as soon as is practicable, and if you should ever decide that you wish to convert to naturism, take up our way of life… don't bother booking."

Unwilling to argue a lost cause, Joe left reception and returned to the chalet where he found Brenda hovering over their small luggage.

"He does have a point, Joe," she said when he told her of the uncomfortable interlude. "Basically, we've done sweet FA other than gather an eyeful of too much flesh."

"Yeah, but it's not like he fed us for free, is it?"

Brenda tutted. "Just forget it. Write it off to experience, and let's get the car loaded and get away from Sun Kissed. I've arranged to meet Sheila near Skegness pier."

Joe did not bother saying 'goodbye' when he dropped the key off, and although Brenda tried to wish the Edströms a fond farewell, they did not answer.

Half an hour later, sat outside a café on Skegness seafront, enjoying the sunshine, Joe was still gloomy, brooding on the money he had (theoretically) lost.

"The thick end of two grand," he grumbled.

Sheila remained philosophical. "There was a time when you didn't charge for your services, Joe. Look upon this as one of those cases."

He scowled. "And we all know who persuaded me to start charging, don't we?" He shook his head. "You know, this is the first time I can remember when I got it all wrong. At other times, even when I did get it wrong, I put it right and fingered the culprit in the end." He checked his watch, and finished his coffee. "Two o'clock. Are we ready to make a move? It's a long drive home."

Brenda's face fell. "Do we have to? We've been so busy at Sun Kissed, that Sheila and I haven't done any shopping."

"And I'm down to the tune of two grand, but duty calls," Joe insisted, "and we're due behind the counter at The Lazy Luncheonette first thing Monday morning."

Sheila gave the matter some thought. "I'm sure Lee, Cheryl, and Kayleigh can manage for one more day. Come on. Why don't we check into a hotel for a couple of nights? It's not going to break the bank is it?"

Joe sighed. "You don't know how close my bank is to breaking, especially now that I'm down two kilos."

Brenda took his hand. "Tell you what, Joe. We'll go Dutch. Sheila and I will pay our way. We can book a double and a single." A sly smile came across her lips. "Sheila can have the single, and I promise you I will take away any depressing thoughts about the money you've lost."

They got to their feet, and began to amble back towards the town.

Sheila chuckled. "Cheer up, Joe. Brenda's just made you a promise."

"On the whole, I'd still rather have the money."

***

A week had gone by when Kirsty rang. It was a Saturday, The Lazy Luncheonette's familiar rush was over and they were winding down to an early finish, as a result of which they were grouped around table five when she rang, and Joe put the call on speaker.

"Just to let you know, Joe, that you were closer to the mark than we realised, and it was Bill Welsby who put us onto it."

"Put you onto what?"

"The Edströms. You accused them of theft and murder, and you got that wrong, but you weren't so far off the mark. When she was in the civil service, Margot worked for immigration, and when he came to this country, Håkan had a bit of a hooky reputation in Scandinavia. Margot cooked the books for him, and he got a new identity and permanent residence. Naturally, we don't know any of this for sure and they're both denying it, but the one thing I can tell you is that they had nothing to do with the murder of Renata Chappell, nor the break in at your chalet. Apparently it was Annaliese who recognised Håkan, and he was their next target."

Concentrating on a minor point, Joe complained, "Margot told me she worked for DEFRA."

"She lied. It happens."

"All right. But what prompted the others to break into our chalet and nick my laptop?"

"Two things. First, you'd already announced yourselves as private eyes and they didn't want you poking your nose in too closely to them. Second – and we got this from Annaliese – on the day you moved in, they saw you carrying a bundle of files, and heard Håkan tell you to take care of them. Data Protection Act. Didn't I tell you the professionals can make a fortune from personal information?"

Joe clucked his annoyance. "So why did they waste Renata?"

"I told you, Annaliese clocked and recognised Edström. They were going to blackmail him until Renata started acting up, talking about going solo. Annaliese waited until Renata went to the ladies and then killed her. With no one else around, it was odds on that Margot would raise the alarm, and bring suspicion on herself. Another blackmail angle. And although it took you a while to get there, you did suspect her. In the meantime Welsby raided your chalet and stashed the files and your laptop in their drum. Easy-peasy until Ellis broke into the Wesley-Simpson chalet and nicked it all again. Welsby and Simpson got Ellis's address from the files and went after him. The rest you know."

Joe put a smile in his voice. "So you got those two and you're chasing the Edströms?"

"Welsby and Simpson bang to rights, but we're not under any pressure to chase up Håkan and Margot. They've not put a foot wrong in the last twenty-five years, but you can take some cred for picking up on them. What is it that your mate Superintendent Cummins says about you? You get the right answer for all the wrong reasons?"

"Don't listen to Terry Cummins. He's jealous of my skill."

Kirsty laughed. "Who wouldn't be?"

Unwilling to get into a different debate, Joe asked. "So what happens to Sun Kissed? Will they be able to pick it up or will Skeggy's naturist park shut down, do you think?"

"We think they'll be fine, and we have heard a whisper that Vivienne Foulkes and Peter Brandon are thinking of putting money into the place. A supplement to their police pensions when they retire." At that, Kirsty brought the discussion to an end. "Anyway, I just thought I'd bring you up to speed. Take care all of you and don't be strangers. There's always a welcome at Skegness cop shop for you."

Joe ended the call and beamed at his two friends. "How about that then? Joe Murray got it right again."

"No you didn't," Brenda insisted.

"Yes I did. I said Håkan and Margot were up to something."

"Yes, but they had nothing to do with any of the crimes we were looking at. Not the thieving, not the murder, none of it."

"Yeah, but they were hooky, the both of them. I don't know how many times I have to tell you, you can't fool me."

Brenda nudged Sheila. "He'll be insufferable all week now."

Sheila agreed. "Can't you keep him occupied?"

Now Brenda laughed. "I try but like most men, he can't stay the pace for long enough."

THE END

The STAC Mystery series:

#1 The Filey Connection
#2 The I-Spy Murders
#3 A Halloween Homicide
#4 A Murder for Christmas
#5 Murder at the Murder Mystery Weekend
#6 My Deadly Valentine
#7 The Chocolate Egg Murders
#8 The Summer Wedding Murder
#9 Costa del Murder
#10 Christmas Crackers
#11 Death in Distribution
#12 A Killing in the Family
#13 A Theatrical Murder
#14 Trial by Fire
#15 Peril in Palmanova
#16 The Squire's Lodge Murders
#17 Murder at the Treasure Hunt
#18 A Cornish Killing
#19 Merry Murders Everyone
#20 A Tangle in Tenerife
#21 Tis The Season To Be Murdered
#22 Confusion in Cleethorpes
#23 Murder on the Movie Set
#24 A Deadly Twixmas

Tales from the Lazy Luncheonette Casebook

By the same author:

#1 A Case of Missing on Midthorpe
#2 A Case of Bloodshed in Benidorm

#1 The Anagramist
#2 The Frame

Fantastic Books
Great Authors

darkstroke is
an imprint of
Crooked Cat Books

- Gripping Thrillers
- Cosy Mysteries
- Romantic Chick-Lit
- Fascinating Historicals
- Exciting Fantasy
- Young Adult
- Non-Fiction

Discover us online
www.darkstroke.com

Find us on instagram:
www.instagram.com/darkstrokebooks

Printed in Great Britain
by Amazon